Cry, the Peacock

This outstanding and compulsive novel by a sensitive writer with vivid imagination and excellent powers of description relates the story of a young girl, Maya, who is obsessed by a childhood prophecy of disaster which cannot be averted. The author builds up an atmosphere of tension as torrid and oppressive as a stifling Indian summer both in the crowded colourful cities and strangely beautiful countryside.

This is also a story of marital discord imbued with a strong streak of neurotic fantasy on the part of woman. The couple, their relatives and friends have been characterized with uncanny precision.

Anita Desai is one of the most distinguished among the younger set of Indo-English writers. She has half-a-dozen novels and collections of short stories to her credit, which include *Voices in the City* and *Bye, Bye, Blackbird*. She was awarded the Sahitya Akademi award in 1978, and the Guardian Award, UK, in 1983.

"Anita Desai creates a stained glass landscape with details of emages, colours and odours...Cry The Peacock is the product of a mellowed craftswoman."
—Statesman

"The author's talent is exceptional in its innate sensibility and awareness of craft of fiction."
—Times of India

GW00673703

Cry,
The Peacock

Anita Desai

ORIENT PAPERBACKS
A Division of Vision Books Pvt Ltd
New Delhi ● Bombay

ISBN-81-222-0085-0

1st Published	1980
Reprinted	1983
Reprinted	1986
Reprinted	1988
Reprinted	1990

Cry, the Peacock

© Anita Desai,1980

Published by
Orient Paperbacks
(A Division of Vision Books Pvt. Ltd.)
Madarsa Road, Kashmere Gate, Delhi-110 006

Printed in India
at Gopsons Paper Pvt. Ltd., Noida

Cover Printed at
Ravindra Printing Press, Delhi-110 006

Part One

All day the body lay rotting in the sun. It could not be moved onto the verandah for, in that April heat, the reek of dead flesh was overpowering and would soon have penetrated the rooms. So she moved the little string bed on which it lay under the lime trees, where there was a cool, aqueous shade, saw its eyes open and staring still, screamed and rushed to the garden tap to wash the vision from her eyes, continued to cry and ran, defeated, into the house. The gardener came and drew its eyelids down with two horny thumbs, reflectively sad as when he laid a dead branch that he had to cut off, on the compost heap. But he would not bury it, as she begged him to do. Often in the course of that day he said to her, patiently, 'The sweeper will do it. He has gone to visit his brother, but when he returns he will do it.' It was afternoon now, and the sweeper had not returned. Crows sat in a circle around the corpse, and crows will eat anything—entrails, eyes, anything. Flies began to hum amidst the limes, driving away the gentle bees and the unthinking butterflies. She thought she saw the evil glint of a bluebottle, and grew hysterical. The gardener sent his wife to take her into the house and keep her there. She sat there, sobbing, and waiting for her husband to come home. Now and then she went out onto the verandah, and looked to see if he were coming up the drive which lay shrivelling, melting and then shrivelling again, like molten lead in a groove cut into the earth, and, out of the corner of her eye, could not help glancing, as one cannot help a tic, at the small white corpse laying at one end of the lawn, under a sheet, under the limes.

Later in the evening, when the sun hung pendent from the topmost branches of the trees, swelling visibly like—she thought—a purulent boil, until it was ripe to drop, her husband came home. He was very late. But as soon as he came, he did all that was to be done, quickly and quietly like a surgeon's knife at work. He telephoned the Public Works Department, he had them send their scavenging truck to take the corpse away, and saw to it himself that they lifted it in with care. 'Yes, yes, the bed too,' he said. 'By all means, burn it too.' When the truck had left, he came to her, wiping his fingers on a handkerchief much used and soiled during the day, yet still in neat folds. 'It is all over,' he said. 'Come and drink your tea, and stop crying. You mustn't cry.'

But she would not lift her face from a cushion, for fear the stench of decaying flesh still hung in the bougainvillaea coloured evening air. All day it had come in with the slow breeze that sucked the curtains in, then slowly drew them out. All day the purple flowers of the bougainvillaeas had cast a flood of coloured shade on her skin; it had been like warm blood bathing her, and could not be washed away. She dared not lift her face to that polluted air, but she asked him, in muffled tones, what he had done.

'I sent it away to be cremated,' he said. 'It is all over. Come, won't you pour out my tea?'

'Tea?' she cried, looking up. 'But ...!' And she

6

stopped still to see that, as every other evening, the tea-tray had been brought to the table beside her, neatly decked with the grandmotherly silver tea-pot, the biscuit tin and the sliced lemon, and the curtains had been drawn as the sun had gone down now, leaving a livid orange glow behind the trees, and all was quiet, formal, waiting.. .just as on every other evening before this. 'Oh !' she cried, helplessly, and ran to the door to see if the bed were not still there, under the limes, but found it gone, and stood there, not knowing where to run next.

'Maya,' he said, patiently. 'Do sit down. You look so hot and worn out. You need a cup of tea.'

'Yes,' she said, sadly, and came back to pour out the tea. But it spilt into the sugar-pot, the tea-strainer toppled into a cup, the lemons slipped to the floor, and there was chaos. Just then the servant came in to announce a visitor—an advocate, he said, come to see the Sahib. And Gautama rose immediately, ordering tea to be sent to the study, forgetting her, forgetting her woes altogether. 'No !' she cried, and fled to the bedroom to fling herself onto the bed and lie there, thinking of the small, still body stiffened into the panic-stricken posture of the moment of death, and of the small sharp yelp in the throat as it suddenly contracted. She did not know it was a scavenger's truck that had taken it away, but she sensed the sordid horror it had brought with it, and left behind, and she began again to cry.

Part Two

1

There remained a certain unease, a hesitance in the air, which kept the tears swimming in my eyes, and prevented their release. I was not allowed the healing passion of a fit of crying that would have left me exhausted, sleep-washed and becalmed. Something slipped into my tear-hazed vision, a shadowy something, that prodded me into admitting that it was not my pet's death alone that I mourned today, but another sorrow, unremembered, perhaps as yet not even experienced, and filled me with this despair. I could not focus my mind upon it, so swiftly and constantly did it move. Lying on my bed with my eyes shut, I tried to think—of the dog rolling over on his back to gaze at me with fond, flower-soft eyes—was it that ? Ah, now that I thought of it, it was, it was indeed, I insisted, clenching my fingers about the pillow. But the pillow, Gautama's, was hard, did not relent, forced me to admit that the strange horror had not yet been recognized even though it was, surely, connected with the corpse, the small, soft corpse and the odour of flesh, once sweet, once loved, then, suddenly, rotten, repulsive. And the liquid brightness of the mirror blurred, the picture went out of focus. I crept into a corner of the bed, crouched there, thinking that it was perhaps because of Gautama not understanding. 'It is all over,' he had said, as calmly as the meditator beneath the *sal* tree. 'You need a cup of tea,' he had said, showing how little he knew of my misery, or of how to comfort me. But then, he knew nothing that concerned me. Giving me an opal ring to wear on my finger, he did not notice the translucent skin beneath, the blue flashing veins that ran under and out of the bridge of gold and jolted me into smiling with pleasure each time I saw it. Telling me to go to sleep while he worked at his papers, he did not give another thought to me, to either the soft, willing body or the lonely, wanting mind that waited near his bed. And now, seeing me bereaved, seeing tears on my face and my pet gone, 'You need a cup of tea,' he said. Yes, I cried, yes, it is his hardness—no, no, not hardness, but the distance he coldly keeps from me. His coldness, his coldness, and incessant talk of cups of tea and philosophy in order not to hear me talk and, talking, reveal myself. It is that—my loneliness in this house. And I clenched my hands again, so that the skin stretched, streams of blood rose and plunged. But when I closed my eyes, they vanished—like the liquid mirror, the black frame of the door, the scarlet blouse flung upon the floor like an abandoned flag. They all dropped from me, disappeared. I was alone. Yes, I whimpered, it is that I am alone, and then gave myself up to a fit of furious pillow-beating, kicking, everything but crying. From childhood experience, I knew this to be sweetly exhausting.

It was exhausting still, but no longer sweetly so. The silence that followed, the stillness, brought my limbs to rest, and my hot face turned at last to the evening breeze coming in at the window, but I realized, also, with new-found maturity, that it was when one's wildest passions were over, one's greatest furies calmed, when the

9

body lay worn and nearly senseless, that one grew most keenly aware of the crepitations of the mind, the strange coldness of the heart, like an expanse of new ice upon which thoughts streaked, distant and dark, haunting one's awareness. I listened to the throb of my pulse. I tried to think of it as the rhythm of a stream which would, if I permitted it, carry me backwards, through scenes and events, flashes of light, cries in the garden, sudden laughter, sudden gusts of wind, to the source of this disturbance. It carried me back, yes, and I thought of Gautama wiping his fingers before he drank his tea, and from there back to my white dog rolling over on his back and inviting me to scratch the rough, sticky fur on his stomach—but no further. There it stuck, was dammed, and I continued to repeat to myself, meaninglessly, the fond names I had had for my pet. Childless women do develop fanatic attachments to their pets, they say. It is no less a relationship than that of a woman and her child, no less worthy of reverence, and agonized remembrance. I shall never forget, I promised, with parted lips and clasped hands, never, and was immediately made aware of the moments trickling past. There was no such thing as never. Only now. And yesterday. To-morrow? Did I need to think of that? I twisted away from tomorrow, because I knew how closely linked to the chain of time was the inevitable order of attach-ment, its disintegration, and then, the deluge.

When Gautama came at last, I had nearly lulled myself to sleep. Abstract thinking never was a great success with me, and I had soon turned to remem-brance of a lullaby that was crooned to me as a child, a gentle, poignant lullaby that I murmured to myself.

So I could turn my face to him without anger, having long since spent it. When he touched my hair, smoothing it down carefully as a nurse would, I was flooded with tenderness and gratitude, thought of him as my guardian, my protector, the one who had seen to the burial of my pet and now came to wipe the strands of hair out of my wet eyes and speak to me softly.

'Lying here in the dark?' he said, and drew a finger down my cheek. Fall, fall, long fall into the soft, velvet well of the primordium, of original instinct, of first-formed love. His tenderness was the cathartic I desired, and now at last I began to cry again, pressing my face against him. 'Come, come,' he said, and took out the handkerchief again, more stained than ever. I clutched it, sobbing. 'Do get up,' he said. 'The servants are coming to take the beds out for the night, and, really, it is much pleasanter outside. Wipe your face, and we'll go out, Maya.' Firmly he helped me out of bed, waited until I had found my slippers and smoothed my clothes, then led me out on the verandah, down the steps into the garden.

It was indeed, as he had promised, much pleasanter there. The balm of darkness met me with a little shock, like a strong and effective medicine on a wound still fresh. I hiccupped. Gautama laughed. This made me feel agreeably like a child; I was not hurt, and I took his arm, even though I knew he detested me to do so. He tolerated my hold for a moment, in consideration of my bereavement, I expect, then moved away, pretending to gesture to the gardener who was sprinkling the lawn so as to lay the dust before the beds were brought out. The rituals of the evening, the preparations for the night, all

11

were vastly comforting to me.

The verandah chairs had been taken out on the lawn for us, two large, comfortable cane chairs, rather battered, rather old, and we sat down, as we did each evening, to glasses of fresh lemonade and to an hour or so of matrimonial silences and conversation. The light in the verandah was on, illuminating the white pillars with an inward glow, as of marble at sunset, though not quite so soft, or quite so translucent. Rangoon creeper entwined these pillars and climbed the walls, spread trembling tendrils towards the roof and wrapped themselves around the gargoyle heads of the drainpipes, choking their grinning mouths with dry leaves, and crowning them with clusters of small, star-like flowers that had been pink and red in daylight, and now were white and strongly scented. They hung in long bunches, like those of white grapes, now rising upon the uneven breeze, now descending, with a slow, mysterious movement as of nocturnal snakes. They say it attracts snakes—this sweet, intoxicating fragrance. No, I am wrong. It is Queen of the Night that attracts snakes. Beauty and evil, evil, beauty. Snakes, summer, scent, flower, white, white, white. . . In the dark, in the dry, scented April dark, the sky was dimly lit by April stars. Winter was over, summer had not yet arrived. I lay back in my chair and breathed deeply, lay there waiting—for summer? for snakes? for the moon? I did not know.

Yes. I did. It was that something else, that indefinable unease at the back of my mind, the grain of sand that irked, itched, and remained meaningless. Meaningless, and yet its presence was very real, and a truly physical shadow, like the giant shadows cast by trees,

12

spilt across the leaves and grasses towards me, with horrifying swiftness, till, like the crowding blades of grass, it reached my toes, lapped my feet, tickling and worrying, and I leapt from my chair in terror, overcome by a sensation of snakes coiling and uncoiling their moist lengths about me, of evil descending from an overhanging branch, of an insane death, unprepared for, heralded by deafening durm-beats. . .

'What is it!' Gautama shouted, jumping too.

'What is it? What is it?' echoed the servants, dropping the sheets that they were spreading on the beds, and coming at a run.

Life, people, light again.

'Nothing, nothing,' I gasped, with my hands to my ears, for it had only been the blood pounding against my ear-drums. Someone switched on a table-lamp, and immediately grass and leaves were lacquered with light; and a large moth came humming along with noisome curiosity, and an owl flew out of the tree, hooting with merriment. 'Nothing,' I repeated, but would not uncover my ears for the blood still beat there, and panic, like a piston, does not cease to live immediately one shuts it off, but continues to beat with a slow, dying rhythm, until it fades naturally away.

Nor would I sit down again. I was poised for flight, prepared for escape, and even though no enemy had revealed itself, I still sharnk from fear of it.

'What was it?' they persisted. 'A frog? A snake?'

'No—nothing, nothing. But I won't sit here. Let us walk, Gautama, let us walk up and down.'

So we did, and the servants went back to sprinkling the lawn, to smoothing sheets, to preparing dinner, and the evening settled back into a familiar routine.

'You are still frightened,' Gautama said, his voice reassuring, logical, calm. 'But why? Now it is all quite over and finished with. He did not really suffer long. If you would like a straw to cling to, then here is one—he did not suffer long. It was over before the vet arrived. The vet would only have prolonged the pain, in a case like this . . .'

'He might have helped,' I whimpered, knowing it had been hopeless.

'But it was hopeless.' Gautama's voice echoing my silent knowledge was like a support to whatever wavered and shook weakly in my wind-swept mind, as it had been on countless similar occasions. As always, it created in me a sensation, a much loved, long courted sensation, of walking through a dark and wet night with somebody beside me who carried a lantern, a staff and a blanket. I moved closer to him, instinctively. 'He told us it had been hopeless,' he said, stopping to light a cigarette. 'I am only sorry about your having been alone with the body all day, with no one to put it away. But by now it must have been cremated. . .'

I drew away from him with a jerk. 'No, stop,' I said, softly. 'Why do you tell me this ?'

He mused for a while, as we walked on, up the lawn, farther apart now than we had been. 'Yes,' he said. 'Why do I? Why do I choose to think of you as one of those mysterious people who find such comfort in hocus-pocus, in the bogus ceremonies and childish trimmings with which we bury our dead? To me, it has always seemed the ultimate absurdity, appropriate only in that it brings a meaningless life to a similarly meaningless end. No doubt the greater per-

centage of those who are buried, or cremated, surrounded by the frills and flaps of pious frivolity, enjoy the
vision of it while alive. Morbidity, you might say but it is
not really that. It is a *belief* in these frivolities. Having
no greater values, they apply themselves with passion to
the lesser ones—which are not values at all, of course,
for values must have a standard, a criterion. . .'

I listened to him, half-attentivelly, half-pensively,
my thoughts straying from the straight, cobbled path
of his march into side-lanes and by-lanes of my own
choosing and my own making, returning now and then
to see if he were still plodding along as he had been
when I deserted him, coming to offer him a handful of
rushes I had collected, or an oddly shaped pebble,
for he was, at times, pleased to accept these offerings
and add them to his subject of conversation as grist
to a mill.

'Why meaningless?' I interrupted him. 'You always
say things like that. As though it didn't matter whether people lived or died.'

'It doesn't,' he snapped. 'Not with the majority of
dim-wits and numbskulls, it doesn't. They are a pack
of sheep in any case. It is only the few who lead these
animals, the ones who are capable of logic and analy-
sis, who matter. Their lives are of importance, and the
triviality of their end is saddening, I admit. Yet I
have known such men—intelligent, reasonable men—
to discuss, with the same avidity the sheep have, the
beauty of burial as opposed to the beauty of cremation,
argue about it as though it were a fine point in theo-
logy. Now this *is* confounding, for these are men who
dedicate themselves to the solidity of thought, of
facts. . .

15

'Burial and cremation are facts, Gautama.'

He shook his head vigorously, in contempt, as though he wished to drive me away from his side. 'Facts that *matter*, I mean, naturally,' he said, in extreme irritation.

Now I was fully with him, following him down the rough cobbles of his straight path. 'But how can you tell which facts matter?' I cried. 'I mean, how can you dictate? Oh, Gautama, pets mightn't mean anything to you, and yet they mean the world to me.' Tears pricked, warm, saline. Danger, danger. I veered away, sobbing a little. 'Living mightn't mean much to some people, but when they die, they want it to happen *splendidly*, something that will be remembered, for ages, by everybody.'

'Ah!' he cried, turning to me, his white face springing out from beneath his hairline, perceptibly, as though to pounce upon something he had recognized, and approved. 'You have done it once again, Maya. You go chattering like a monkey, and I am annoyed that I have been interrupted in my thinking. But, being a creature of instinct, you do, every now and then, stumble—purely by accident, I'm sure— upon the salient point of the problem, the very solution, in this case. They want something that will be remembered! The desire for immortality! Ah,' he said, and hastily lit another cigarette to enhance his delight. 'Now what is there in the ancient rites of cremation that is worth remembering? A wealthy *zamindar* might introduce novelties into his house, to impress, fashionable motor cars. But he will not deviate from tradition when it comes to birth, marriage or death. Oh no. And why? Bedause he knows, and

16

even the worst fool will accept this truth, by sheer force of persistence, that the only thing that continues to live is tradition. Not every tradition, ancient as it might be—and that is why we always have the antediluvian sector amidst the older generation that spends its time in vociferously mourning bygone ways—but those that have certain reasons, and have proved, by time, to be durable. Having endured, they must be worthy of endurance, claim these simple souls, and thus they find something they can dedicate their small silly minds to with impunity.'

'It is also because it *matters* to them,' I insisted, my attention having been held so long through sheer pleasure in the compliment he had paid me. Not, perhaps, a compliment in the sense that it would have been one whichever woman it was paid to, but, coming from him, to me, it was one, and I had learnt its value.

'That is not the point' he said, snapping his teeth sharply. 'As I have pointed out, their criterion is no criterion at all. Why *should* it matter? It doesn't— not only because their lives are trivial and expendable in any case, but also because our religion trains us not to believe in these empty rites. The *Gita* does not preach involvement in tradition. It preaches—reco- mmends, rather—detachment on every count. If only those who read it so piously, in front of their plaster gods, every morning and every night, would also understand it, then they would be capable of disappear- ing without drawing down upon their heads this paraphernalia of vulgarity at the very moment of their disappearance.'

Disappearance? Ah no, not that. It was a cruel

17

word, cruelly spoken, and I felt a pang as the solidity of real existence gave forth one little gasp and collapsed, like a worm-eaten fruit, at my feet. At any rate, this was what Gautama's words implied I could not believe him. I thought of Toto's short stump of a white tail again, of the foolish little wisp at its end. And of his wild, thrilled bark as he saw me return from a morning in town, the impact of his body as he flung himself upon me. These did not—disappear. Not meaninglessly. They were at least as enduring as the "facts" Gautama was continually extolling. Were they not? I pleaded silently, childishly. Were they not? But I did not ask aloud. These were private thoughts and having thought them was sufficient. And I had to learn to be grateful for his presence alone, not be disturbed by the meanderings of his brain which, when with me, worked like a clock spring unwinding itself into relaxation.

And so we strolled up and down the lawn, talking desultorily, not really listening to each other, being intent, on our own paths which, however, ran parallel and closely enough for us to briefly brush against each other, now and then, reminding us—or, perhaps only myself—of the peace that comes from companion life alone, from brother flesh. Contact, relationship, communion... I let these warm, tender sensations bathe me in their lambency, soothe me till the disturbed murmurs of my agitation grew calmer, and I could step out of the painful seclusion of my feelings into an evening world where the lawn had just been trimmed, the flower-beds just watered. The season for flowers was over now—had disappeared—but no, not quite, not in entirety. There were still some

18

beds of petunias, floppy white and faint mauve petunias—sentimental, irresolute flowers, I always felt, and yet, at dusk, they emitted such a piercing swoon of scent, a poignant, half-sweet, half-sad fragrance that matched my mood to perfection, and I started to it with the embrace of recognition, taking in deep breaths of this gentle, fading odour that was so laden with wistful remembrance of the winter, a sense of all good things having come to an end, and only the long, weary summer to look forward to. . .a Sunday evening sense that precedes each tedious Monday.

I ventured to speak of this to Gautama. He sniffed the air. Like a horse, he raised his head, pointed his chin, and sniffed the air. He had not noticed anything himself, never did. 'Ah,' he said, having sniffed. 'Yes and the lemons also'.

'Oh no,' I cried dismayed. 'Not at all!' The blossoms of the lemon tree were different, quite different: of much stronger, crisper character, they seemed cut out of hard moon shells, by a sharp knife of mother-of-pearl, into curving, scimitar petals that guarded the heart of fragrance. Their scent, too, was more vivid—a sour, astringent scent, refreshing as that of ground lemon peel, a crushed lemon leaf. I tried to explain this to Gautama, stammering with anxiety, for now, when his companionship was a necessity. I required his closest understanding.

How was I to gain it? We did not even agree on which points, on what grounds this closeness of mind was necessary. 'Yes, yes,' he said, already thinking of something else, having shrugged my words off as superfluous, trivial, and there was no way I could make him believe that this, the night filled with

19

these several scents, their varying essences and associations, their effects on me, on us, were all important, the very core of the night, of our moods tonight.

'Oh, Gautama,' I said, and sighed in resignation, for we had been married four years now—'No, you are too young!' people sometimes cried, and, turning to a mirror, I agreed it was hard to believe, and yet it was true, and four years it had been—and I had developed a slightly greater capacity for philosophy than I was born with. 'You notice nothing at all,' I sighed. 'What *are* you thinking of? That man who came to see you this evening? He kept you in the office for an hour—or more, I'm sure. What did he want? Oh, you don't need to tell me—it must have been about some musty old case, about money, or property, or something dreary like that. Wasn't it?

'Money? Well yes, if we must be so basic.'

'But of course we must, Though I'm sure I don't know if money is basic. And why must it always be money? It's always money, or property—never a case of passion and revenge, murder, and exciting things like that—basic things. Why? Don't they ever happen?'

'Murder ? Yes, that happens, indeed it does.'

'Yes, but only for the sake of money, or property—or anything solid, and dirty. Not for love, or life, or *basic* things—like Toto dying. Toto. . .'

Quickly he interrupted, his words cutting my thoughts away like a surgeon expertly removing a boil. 'In other words,' he said swiftly, 'you feel the world will die for what is known to us as reality, not for ideals. Like most young people, you cannot understand that reality and idealism are one and the same thing. Life is not a matter of distinguishing between

20

the two, but of reconciling them. But, in such matters, we are all opsimaths, and one day you shall learn that these ideals eventually resolve themselves into realities one has known all one's life, and spurned perhaps. Love—that great and splendid ideal of the young—ultimately becomes, you will find, for the man a matter or dealing with the bills that come in, and, for the woman, of worrying about them. Or, if you choose, of rearing chidren and paying for their rearing. It does not change as such, but merely reveals another facet. As for death—Toto's dying, you will find, will become a matter of missing the games you played with him, finding empty time heavy on your hands and, ultimately, a search for a replacement. It is rather shocking to reduce one's ideals to mundane superfluities, and equally shocking to realize that these superfluities are the ideals themselves. . .'

So rambling, he drew me away from my thoughts of anguish which rose, every now and then, like birds that awake from dreams and rise out of their trees amidst great commotion, circle a while, then settle again, on other branches. We walked towards a stone urn filled with white petunias that stood in the centre of the lawn, and here I paused, for, in their presence, I was drawn away from [pain into a world that knew no pain. To draw as close as possible to the heart of that mystery was to draw close to its lovely solution. I bent over them, inhaling that mist of sad, maidenly scent, feeling mood merge into mood, sensation into sensation, till there was nothing left but that mist.

Gautama stopped also. He had no use for flowers, but he threw back his head and said; 'What a clear night' and, unbending, I looked up too, and higher

21

up. The stars surged towards us, their whole diamond weight descending upon us. More and more stars rushed into our scope of vision, new ones seemed to burst into birth, dying ones to revive. And yet, no matter how many the enchanted eye gathered, there were still spaces of darkness in between, above and around, and it was that which gave the air such weight, I found, and not the myriad stars. Death lurked in those spaces, the darkness spoke of distance, separation, loneliness—loneliness of such proportion that it broke the bounds of that single word and all its associations, and went spilling and spreading out and about, lapping the stars, each one isolated from the other by so much. And the longer I gazed, the farther they retreated, till there was only the darkness hanging, like a moist shroud, over our heads, and I thought of the long journey of the dead from one birth into another, the brave traversing of mute darkness, the blind search for another realm of lucidity in the midst of chaos. And I looked down again, and fingered one soft-petalled flower, a white one. Small white Toto, whining a little, out of fear, his futile barks dying away into a hopeless silence. Small white Toto, small white corpse in the blaze of sun, abandoned. 'I shall miss him so—terribly, Gautama,' I cried then, the confession tearing out of me in a stormy rush, and even as I wiped away my quick tears, and wept more, I cried to myself—What is the use ? I am alone·

But I was not, for Gautama heard, and not only that, but he raised his hand to wipe a tear away, his hand as cool and dry as the bark of an old and shady tree. He quoted, softly, an Urdu couplet.

22

'Even if each star in the sky were an heart, what of it ?

Give to me one heart that is capable of sorrow.'

Shooting-star, rocket, comet, great fountain of light, light, diamond, brilliant, sapphire light. Darkness, chaos—gone And I spun around to face him, this visitant to what had seemed a pit of black emptiness, as the night hurtles towards a falling star, clinging to its traces. He had already put his hands behind his back, was already walking away restlessly, already, musing upon 'A new book Professor Rehman sent me today, one of his publications—a very distinguished anthology of Persian couplets, though it has, perhaps, a trifle too much of the last century, a trifle too little of contemporary work . . .'

I did not listen to these words, I heard that couplet alone, that couplet, weighted with a rare compassion, a tender understanding, so that it hung pendent in the dark like a radiant rain-drop, catching the starlight, catching it and flashing, brighter and brighter. And my heart stretched, stretched painfully, agonizingly, expanding and swelling with the vastness of a single moment of absolute happiness, and my body followed its long, sweet curve, arching with the searing, annihilating torture of it. Ultimate. A word dropped down the tall tunnel of memory—it had been used that evening—Ultimate. Ah, this was it, the ultimate, absolute joy. Here lay perfection, suspended, bearing all that it could bear, so full was it. Were one more flower to unfurl that night, one small bird to cry, if one bright star were to be shattered and fall now—I could not have borne it, no. I was filled, filled to the point of destruction. God, God, I gasped—enough, enough, no

23

more. Let it remain so. Let it remain. . .

And then that breath was released, a new one drawn. The agony of it.

I insisted we leave the lights off in the diningroom, that we eat by the light that meagrely came in through the open doors of other rooms, imagining that from this dimness we should be able to look out on the stars.

'They are *so* bright tonight,' I pleaded.

'Well, I hope bright enough for me to spot a fly if it falls into my dinner,' grumbled Gautama, who was no romantic, and, having quoted, forgot the content of the quotation which I, rapturously, continued to turn over and over in my mind, as a child clutches and fondles a wonderful toy.

Somehow the darkness killed our appetites. Gautama, complaining that it was too hot to eat, smoked between courses, and I, my tongue thick and unsavoury from having cried so much, concentrated on a salad of pomelos and chillies, sadly reflecting that, on another day, this vision of crisp pink fruit speckled with fresh green would have illuminated an entire evening. But tonight we were subdued. One could only see a few pale stars glimmering low over the trees, not many, from the wide open windows through which no breeze entered.

And finally, when a clumsy, fluttering moth did fall into the iced sweet on Gautama's plate, I rose and switched on the lights resignedly, begging him not to shout so. The stars were a failure.

That night Gautama worked late. I went to bed alone, carrying my glass of water which I set down on the little table between our beds, which were two rectangles of immaculate white on the inky lawn at the back of the house. A row of papaya trees behind them, a tangle of vines—beans, jasmine, all mixed—hid the servants quarters from view. But it did not shut out the sound of their voices, or of the small drum someone was thumping, or the chant of 'Radha-krishna, Radha-Krishna...' a lulling, soothing chant. I sat down on my bed, cool and refreshed after a bath, in my white night-clothes, and began to feel more at peace. I knew a special technique of getting into bed on summer nights, and took a deep skindiver's breath before I lay down, very slowly stretched out one leg, then the other, first one arm, then the next, slowly let my breath out in a long sigh, and collapsed onto the cool, smooth sheets with delicious abandon. Very slowly I uncurled my fingers and toes so that they, too, were completely relaxed... 'Like a cat,' Gautama had said, smiling, during the earlier days of our marriage when he was still capable of such amative whimsicalities: 'A small, lazy cat'...Quietly I breathed the night in, letting the rhythm of the chant wash over me in swift, regular waves. Night, night, deep, dark night. This, I knew, was what one lived for: the nights were always beautiful—the gentle herbal balm rubbed into the hot temples and fevered bruises inflicted by the long, frustrating day. Night and stars, newly discovered splendour of stars. There they were, a diamond frieze, low above me. The sky was intensely black, intensely soft, so that one's eyes plunged and pierced, but, awed, soon foundered and clung to the stars instead—the large, calm stars with names to them that I did not know, and rings of milky luminescence around them that glowed, and the smaller, nameless ones that winked on and off, on and off, so fast that the dazzled eye could never note the instant when they were off. The Milky Way swooped across from north-east to south-west *Akash—Ganga,* the Ganges of the sky. I lay there, thinking of the stars that composed that great, pale girdle that bound horizon to horizon, of the immense distance between earth and stars, of the millions of years, the aeons that it took for their light to travel down the great vacuum into my waiting eyes. A shooting-star sped across the sky, then disintegrated into sparks that were immediately extinguished.

I twisted uneasily. The peace I had prepared for, ritual-fashion, had not descended after all, and my line of thought made me restless, not calm. Like a magic charm, I repeated Gautama's couplet to myself, the lovely words, trying to think of their richness and tenderness alone. But it did not help. I twisted around farther still, staring at the big papaya leaves behind my head that were like Chinese paper-cuts silhouetted against the lush night sky. I tried to concentrate on the voices that droned 'Radha-Krishna, Radha-Krishna' in a bemused rhythm, and found it only transported me back to the awareness of the loneliness of time, the impossible vastness of space. Where did I stand in it ? In these decades that were spelt out in flashing hieroglyphs above my head ?

For there never was a doubt in my mind, now that I remember, as to the definite truth that I did indeed have a place in it. Not only I, but my small dog, whose sad journey I followed with my mind, even as my eye traced pattern after majestic pattern amidst the proud constellations.

Gautama—I should have liked to call out to him.

26

I turned to the light in his study, a small bright oblong in the silent house. It would be long before he shut his books and came to me. Dared I go in ? Beg for comfort ? Confess to my loneliness and my terror of loneliness ? Useless. Hopeless. From my twisted position, I sank back into relaxation, shut my eyes, and immediately opened them again—bright pin-pricks probed them open. And it was not only the stars but that strange unease that had troubled me all day. A persistent sense of some disaster I had known, and forgotten, or perhaps never known, only, at one time, feared, and now rediscovered. But what was it ? A grain of sand itching, itching upon the tender infant skin of my new sorrow. Yet no mere grain. Far more important. Not merely a foreboding, but a distant apprehension of a presence. Like an under-current beneath the throbbing of drums, a foreign odour amidst the scent of lemon blossoms, a struggle of despair that continued beyond the sleep of death. I searched the stars, unhappily, fearsomely even. I could not shut my eyes upon them—tonight they had a fascination that was no longer one of pure enchantment. It was as though I were faced with an important message in a language I could not read. Thinking now of Toto, then of a growing desire to call Gautama, and ultimately of whatever I knew of the constellations, I sifted through the hieroglyphs. It was a language I had once known, I needed only to remember. But I must do so soon. How ? Why ? And after that—what ?

In the end, it was not the stars that told me, but the moon, when it rose out of the churn of my frenzy, vast and ghost-white, written over with dim, tortuous signs in ashgrey, casting a searing shaft of stark white across my body which thereupon began to shake, for it was not the gentle moon of love ballads and fairy revels that so swiftly mounted the roof of our house, but a demoniac creature, the fierce dancer that had all day been trying to leap the threshold of my mind and home, accompanied by a deafening roar of silent drums. It was the mad demon of Kathakali ballets, masked, with heavy skirts swirling, feet stamping, eyes shooting beams of fire. It was a phantom gone berserk, and, from a body of absolute white, assumed terrible colours, rose out of realms of silence into one of thunderous drumming.

God! God! I cried, and sat up in terror. There was no clash and clamour after that. I was aware of a great, dead silence in which my eyes opened to a vision that appeared through the curtains of the years, one by one falling back till I saw again that shadow. A black and evil shadow. Its name was not that of a demon in a Kathakali dance drama, nor was it one of the limpid appellations of the moon. It was, I remembered it now, Fate.

He had been—large or small? I cannot remember, but his eyes I do : they were pale, opaque, and gave him an appearance of morbidity, as though he had lived, like a sluggish white worm, indoors always, in his dark room at the temple gates, where the central lingam was painted a bright, vicious red, as though plunged in sacrificial blood, and light burned in a single lamp from which oil spilled into a large, spreading pool. Just as his shadow spread and spread, a stain edging towards me who stood, clutching my *ayah's* hand, in paralyzed terror and even fiercer fascination, my toes curling away from the oil, from his

28

shadow. 'Not only here, but in your horoscope also,' he said, tapping the long chart the *ayah* had had made for me, 'and there, on your forehead too,' he smiled, and, laying down the paper, he raised his hand, a plump, oiled hand with dyed nails, bringing it close to my face so that I felt as though a bat were caught in the same room with me, and shrank involuntarily. But he lowered it without touching me and turned to finger the horoscope instead, its minute figures and designs. 'Just as it is prophesied here, I see it there,' he smiled. 'Unmistakably.' He offered me lemonade, he offered the *ayah* tea. We refused, I froze, the *ayah* began to complain, suddenly, as though she had developed an uncomfortable itch somewhere. He smiled at us, continuously. He came near me again, his shadow lapped me, playfully, flirtatiously 'There, between the eyes—the exact spacing... Marvellous—who would have thought—?' he mused, and the madly blank eyes were glazed. He begged me be seated, be patient. He twitched the fold of his grimy robe between thighs that flashed through holes and openings, here, there, obscenely. 'No doubt about it, and so it is my duty to warn you.' Like sweet oil, his smiles dripped on me. 'My child, I would not speak of it if I saw it on your face alone. But look, look at the horoscope. Stars do not lie. And so it is best to warn you, prepare you.' He played on in this manner, seemed even pleased when the *ayah*, grown impatient and plaintive, interrupted with her whinings, her protests, for this gave him time to argue with her, coyly, and prolong the tense drama. All the while he smiled, and his eyes now turned colourless, now flashed with light. Sometimes he grew emphatic, and creased

29

his brow, and raised his arms, his voice. 'Death,' he finally admitted, in one such moment, 'to one of you. When you are married—and you shall be married young.' The light suddenly sank, and his eyeless face assumed the texture of a mask above me. 'Death—an early one—by unnatural causes,' he said, softly, sibilantly, and gently lowered his arms till they dropped to his side, then became furiously mobile once more, casting his robes once this way, once that. He cut short the *ayah's* horrified wail. 'Be quiet, woman, who speaks to you, you old illiterate? You believe me anyhow, whether I lie or speak the truth. But the child—the child must be persuaded, she must listen to my warning. It is my duty to prepare her, my duty.' He approached me again, with dancing steps, when the weak flame of the single lamp suddenly guttered and died. We all sprang up, and the darkness was filled with crowding, pushing, grasping bodies, moist with perspiration, reeking with evil, the emanation and apprehension of it. 'Oil,' he cried. 'I shall fetch some oil,' and the *ayah* screamed, 'No, fool, there is oil enough, too much of it— it has drowned the wick,' and then I found the door, flung it open, thinking to meet a great rush of daylight and sanity. But the door opened onto a courtyard shaded by a vast tree, and the light was subdued, grey. But light it was, and by its help the woman lit the lamp again, having squeezed the wick dry between her fingers. I saw the floor littered with ants, and corpses of ants that had come to drink the sweet oil and drowned in it. I had only time to note this, nothing more, when he shut the door again, quickly, with the albino's dread of light, and slyly, behind my back. He chuckled, gnomishly. 'Now we can go back to our very important conversation,' he said. 'Of course you are still so young, so very young'—flicking the fold of his robe over his loins, flicking it—'there is still so much time. Or have arrangements already been made—for a marriage?' 'No!' I shouted. 'I will never marry,' and at the same time the *ayah* screamed, 'Give me that horoscope you have made—lies, all lies. Give it to me so we can leave now.' And he raised his hands, rolled his eyes, crying, 'Calm yourselves! Calm yourselves!' But we were in a frenzy now—I rushed to the door, the *ayah* seized the scroll. He grew perturbed, peremptory. 'Sit down,' he said, sternly, in a voice of steel. 'Listen to me, women,' he snapped, like a whip, 'For there is only a chance, a faint possibility that her life should take this path. The sign is there. The stars prophesy it. But we are in the hands of God,' and here his voice dropped, softened, began to quiver with emotion. He lived behind the temple, heard the bells and saw the worshippers supplicate. 'God guides us all. He may guide you onto another path, if you pray for it to be so, offer sacrifices in order that it may be so.' He had a rosary. 'God guides you, child,' he murmured, close to my ear, and chanted a prayer opening his eyes wide and rolling them so that the iris formed white circles that gleamed around the pale pupils. 'Four years after your marriage, so the stars prophesy, and the space between your eyes, the mark there, supports this prophecy I have warned you, performed my duty. Be wary, child, be wary and fear God. Worship Him, make sacrifices. Pray. Do we not know, all of us here, the story of Prahlad? Of how Krishna saved him again, and again, countless times, through

31

love and mercy? Have not all heard of how Prahlad was flung from the mountain top and Krishna caught him in his arms? Of how he was flung into a fire. . .' The entire encounter ended in tales of mythology, in some philosophy, much contorted even to my infantile ears, in prayers and songs, religious songs, till the sticky net of his shadow at last slipped away and released me, and I was able to open the door and make my old *ayah* take me home, away from this fearsome magician—for that is what I called him, a magician. And he ushered us out, flicking the garment that slipped about his hips, flicking it as a lizard flicks its tongue at a petrified victim, and than hastily drew back into the shadows before a stray ray of light could strike him with its purifying glare of whiteness.

The moon did her utmost. With sweet, pale coolness, she shone and shone, turning all that was grey to either black or white, so that suspicious half-tones, disturbing shades all vanished, and there was no gloom left. Nor was it white heat at all, I found, but cooling menthol, a lucid balm that bathed my tingling skin. But it was a sharp, penetrating balm, for not only did it play upon me and wash me, but it pierced my body and surged through my veins so that my blood ran to its calling, rose to my brain, and I was in a fever. It was all so clear now, so magically clear. . . the disturbing memory, half-remembered, had turned to a vision of albino eyes, of dyed finger nails pointing at my forehead, at the stars, and its reality was as unmistakable as that of the white moon. And four years it was now, we had been married four years. It was as though the moonlight had withered the shadows in my mind as well, leaving it all dead-white, or dead-black. When the drums fell silent and the moon began to sink over the trees, I knew the time had come. It was now to be either Gautama, or I.

When at last he came out to sleep, I could not speak to him, but lay still, pretending to be asleep.

2

Gautama gave me a cat. She was white and had hair like tassels of silk. Her large almond eyes were topaz, with undertones of grey and overtones of green. Gautama said she must surely have been a Chinese mandarin in a previous existence. Her sense of the valuable and the lovely was of an unbelievable quality. She would follow me into the garden, on fastidiously stepping paws, and delicately sniff the blooms. When I bent a perfumed poppy or oleander towards her, she would tilt her face to it. She would sit long hours on the verandah steps, gazing at the moon. This was a fascination we shared, and I thought to found a friendship upon it, but she scorned to have me touch her secret dreams. She was exquisite, and disdained my sudden movements, my loud chatter. We tiptoed around each other with great caution, and, sometimes—in brief, breathless moments—we came close enough to touch.

By then it was Spring. As ever, Spring came with the brain-fever bird, whose long, insistent call rang imploringly from the tree-tops all morning and, again, at twilight. I woke each morning to its call, the first sound of dawn, as it begged, 'Who are you? Who are you?' in that early peach light that ripened to bronze-on-fire before we even rose, to breakfast on tea and papayas sprinkled with lemon and sugar. It was an untidy season for spring was combined with the qualities of autumn, and trees shed leaves even as new ones grew tumescent, for there was no winter to freeze the bare twigs and keep the fecund sap in frigid hibernation—only the quickening, pulsing heat that impassioned the spawning roots. Leafless, the fine tracery of the naked *neem* trees revealed unsuspected, so far carefully concealed, nests, deserted by the birds once they were bared to the sight of little boys on the streets who held stones, missiles, ever-ready, in their hot fists. Appearing bigger than they were in reality, because of their singularity, they looked sad, scraggy— baskets formed of the leaves and berries of more fruitful seasons that held the fading flowers and con- tented yawns of a mild, sweet winter. Pariah kites soared high in the sky that had paled from the cold weather's intense cobalt to an effete, milk-washed blue, and their high, piercing calls came whistling down on whorls of air that also caught the fine, powdery dust and turned it into a host of cavorting spooks along the roads. Down the street the silk-cotton trees were the first to flower : their huge, scarlet blooms, thick-petalled, solid-podded, that made blood-blobs in the blue, then dropped to the asphalt and were squashed into soft, yellowish miasma, seemed animal rather than flowerage, so large were they, so heavy, so moist and living to the touch. Their pods were crowded with silk cotton and, as they burst, these airy- faery puffs of sliver-streaked whiteness were released and sailed through the air like angelic, soft-feathered birds, and rolled along the streets in radiant billows till the dust soiled them. Children picked them up and blew

34

them up in the air, and old women gathered them into sacks to sell to manufacturers of pillows and babies' quilts.

On our verandah, the pigeon's nests were suddenly filled with babies that twittered and muttered and whispered and whimpered all day. The floor was littered with their droppings and discarded twigs. Other springs, I had had ladders propped up, and climbed them to peep at these minute, peeping infants. This year I was exasperated by them. The doves, in a mood for mating, cooed to each other until I was distracted. I counted them as omens of ill fortune, of separation, for their coo was a tedious repetition of the fatal words, 'Go away!' All day they repeated their warning, and I longed to drive them away, yet dared not disturb their amour.

The atmosphere was charged with restlessness, as my hair, suddenly grown drier and finer, was charged with electricity and crackled sharply when I brushed it. Gusts of wind dragged the thorny, paper-flowered bougainvillaea creepers against the wall with a dry, scratching rattle that unnerved me. The cries of birds, caught in the rut of love, were like frantic warnings to my ears. The rolling cotton-balls, the flying yellow leaves, the surging clouds of dust, all seemed to flee, flee, flee, and yet could not, for they were bound to the season, and returned to continue their struggle for escape. Something similar heaved inside me—a longing, a dread, a search for solution, a despair, and my head throbbed and spun as I lay flat on my back through the long afternoons, under the fan that turned, turned relentlessly, and sent a small quivering breeze over my body, blowing my hair across my damp face, then blowing it away again. When

35

Gautama returned from work, took me out, spoke to me and led me to a certain calm, then the brain-fever bird would begin again her mournful cry, upsetting me so violently that I would not be able to sleep all night.

Gautama said, 'It is the spring.'

It is another spring—a far more idyllic one, for it is at home, in Lucknow. I have been strolling amidst the vegetables with father—he takes an interest in tomatoes of a foreign variety, and I nibble at a radish, then a sprig of dill—but he has been called in by a visitor, and now I am waiting for him, in the shade of the bougainvillaea arbour, where the light turns from lilac to mauve to purple, from peach to orange to crimson, as the small whispers of breeze turn and turn again the heavy load of blossoms upon the air. I see the sky through them, and the vast lawn stretching out towards the creeper-hung bungalow, and all the world is tinted like sweet sherbet. I stretch out my naked legs, and blades of grass are crushed under them, then spring up again with an even stronger odour of milk and cows and honey. I watch a small butterfly flicker amongst the flowers : it has white wings, each with an orange fleck. Bright and fluttering, it is as much of a gay paper-cut as the flowers. The world is like a toy specially made for me, painted in my favourite colours, set moving to my favourite tunes.

But my eyes tire of the sun and brightness. I roll over on my stomach, and kick up my legs and gaze into the deep, serene green of the grass, lush enough to graze in, drown in. I close my eyes and listen to the shrilling of ecstatic insects—ecstatic because it is the season of hot quivering sun, and they thrive on it.

36

The tremulous, flower-tinted air is vibrant as a violin string set into motion by the fine, tender leg of a brilliant grasshopper. High, incessant sounds form out of the very sun and air on such a morning, like crystals in syrup. Delight makes me drowsy. When I open my eyes, I see one of those small, round, red insects that I call "velvet bugs" for they are of the texture and colour of the thick rich velvet on our settee in the drawing-room. It is perched on the sharp tip of a blade of grass which bends with its tiny weight. It can be no more comfortable than I would be were I set upon the tip of a sabre, and so I lift it off with my little finger, and hold it there, stroking it, very gently, with another finger. I hum a song to please it. I lay it back on the grass to see it glow, ember-red, ruby-like on the lawn. My father has shown me just such a ruby, only the other night, taking it out of the safe on a white pad, to tell me it will be mine when I am old enough to attend my first grown-up party, if only I will stop crying . . . When was that ? What made me cry so ? I forget, and quickly grope for this live ruby in the grass, cradle it in my hands. It is so marvellous, so worthy of my most concentrated attention, that the whole morning fades into the shade of the arbour and even the voices coming from the portico are perceived by my ears, but barely impressed on my mind.

Yet, they are clear enough. And surprising. For it is father saying, 'I do not wish to see you anywhere in the city again,' in a tone that is harsh, peremptory. 'I have ordered your removal, and my own friends in the police force will see to it. Attempt a return, and I shall have you put in prison. Charlatan. Charlatan.' These words are like the knocking of a hoopoe's long bill into the dry bark of a dead silver oak tree, as it drives the panicstricken insects around to the other side of the tree-trunk, then darts around in a flash of black and scarlet and gold, to quickly gobble them up. 'Charlatan. I shall have you put in prison for life— you and that foolish woman together, do you hear?'

Another voice replies loudly, querulously, in complaint, or pleading, like a brain-fever bird, and, for a brief instance, I awake to it, frowning, for a nerve within me has been touched that was touched before, and is still raw, from the bruise. Was it that that had made me cry? When? Who was it? I wonder. The little bug topples over on its back, and I quickly bend to search for it, losing interest in everything else, though I hear the hammer continue to beat harshly: 'Charlatan. Is this not enough? Have you not heard?' It thunders on, and then the buzz of honey bees and dragonflies' wings softens and subdues it into the sweet, inconsequential oumbling of this ecstatic morning basking in the sun.

I hear footsteps disappear down the gravel of the long drive, but can see no one for the silver oak trees thickly line the way, their grey leaves turning in the breeze to reveal undersides of silver down. They are in flower, and their flowers are bristles of gold. Gold and silver. Starlings come in flocks to feed upon them—pink flocks, black-flecked.

'Maya!' my father calls, and it is in a voice so different from the one that had spat out 'Charlatan,' that perhaps it was not his voice at all that I had heard. 'Maya.' I answer him so that he might find me. I wish to show him my velvet bug, but it is lost, gone. However, there are various other delights to distract me from that loss, and I point out the starlings

38

to him. He notices a dead branch on one of the silver oaks and, with a small muscle at the corner of his mouth twitching—for he is particular about the garden —he complains of the laziness of the gardener. We go in search of him amongst the vegetables. I hold his arm. He pats it briefly, distractedly.

'Who was that?' I ask. 'Who was that talking to you just now?'

He starts a bit, then beams at me. Since my *ayah* left, so suddenly, the other day, without even wishing me good-bye, he has looked after me alone, and his beam is especially tender, his attention especially loving. I think that he is like a silver oak himself, with his fine, silver-white hair brushed smoothly across his bronzed scalp. He is dressed in white. His eyes are half-closed to the sun, and small crinkles radiate from their corners. I hug his arm tightly, for I have always loved, instinctively, anyone who crinkles the corners of his eyes when he smiles. To me, it is a sign of warm-heartedness of tenderness, and reminds me, always, of this man's open love for me.

'Why do you ask?' he says lightly. 'What would it mean to you if I told you of a naughty clerk, or a lying client ?'

'I would—I would hit him with my tennis racket!'

He laughs loudly, for this is the kind of remark that, coming from me, pleases him inordinately. People say he spoils me. This means that he fondles my cheek, holds my hand, and says to me, 'It is getting warm. Time for us to retreat to the hills, isn't it ? Where shall we go this year, Maya ? Choose !' People say he spoils me. They also say that I can get anything I want from him. 'Darjeeling !' I cry, jubilantly. 'Of

39

course !' and jump up and down at his side.

'If only we could go away for the summer,' I sighed, lethargically, breaking my promise never to say such things to Gautama who had never been able to "go away for the summer" till he married me, and then refused to do so. It was discouraging to reflect on how much in our marriage was based upon a nobility forced upon us from outside, and therefore neither true nor lasting. It was broken repeatedly, and repeatedly the pieces were picked up and put together again, as of a sacred icon with which, out of the pettiest superstition, we could not bear to part.

Gautama's reaction was exactly what I might have predicted, had I throught before speaking. Immediately he stiffened, turned from me and picked up the papers. 'Why don't you ?' he said, in a cold, astringent tone. 'Your father would take you wherever you wanted to go. He *can*.' It was the tone he normally used in speaking of my father, but without any leavening of indulgence. Yet they had been friends—Gautama almost a protégé of my father, who had admired him and, I believed, still did. Coming slowly up on his bicycle, in the evenings, it was my father Gautama used to come to call upon, and had it not been for the quickening passion with which I met, half-way, my father's proposal that I marry this tall, stooped and knowledgeable friend of his, one might have said that our marriage was grounded upon the friendship of the two men, and the mutual respect in which they held each other, rather than upon anything else. To watch this respect being broken, reduced or, at any rate, concealed, at a steadily growing rate, by Gautama, had been almost the most searing pain of the first year of our marriage, especially as I knew that I was, in some way, responsible for it. But now I had a headache, such a fierce headache, I really could not bear to worry about it any longer.

'Ah, Gautama,' I cried, tearfully, and rose from my pillows to hold and draw him into my own orbit of thought and feeling, yet not daring to make the bold, physical move. 'You don't imagine I would go without you ? Leaving you behind in the heat ?'

'Why not ?' he said, snapping open his cigarette case with a metallic click that matched his voice. 'I daresay I can manage, considering I did so for a great many years before I married you.'

'Don't,' I cried, writhing, 'please don't speak like that.'

'Don't speak like what, in God's name ?' he said. He spoke in exasperation now. Danger!

I lay back in bed. 'You know I wouldn't', I said, staring at his back with its bent spine and projecting ribs that I would have stroked as eagerly as I would have fondled the cat's soft fur, had I seen her arch her lovely head, or touched a rind of melon that invited by its granulated, green-ribbed coarseness. I should have liked to reach out and touch, gently, one curving rib. Nothing could have disgusted him more, at this moment, in such a mood, and knowing this, I started to run my fingers distractedly through my hair instead. 'Is there so much work to be done this summer? Couldn't you get away—just for a short holiday?'

His cigarette calmed him. He blew spirals of blue smoke into the dimness of the shuttered room. 'Unlikely,' he said. 'There *is* a lot of work,' and he turned his head to look at me. I turned upon my side, closer to him, conscious of the swell of my hip that rose under the white sheet which fell in sculptured folds about my rounded form. His eyes remained blank of appraisal, of any response. It was as though he had seen only what he had expected to see, nothing less, and nothing more. What cause for excitement than? He said, 'Where would you like to go? Darjeeling?'

'Father would be there,' I confessed, and felt something spring up amidst my crushed spirits, like fresh grass after rain.

'I thought as much,' he said, smiling the smile that meant nothing more than a little cynicism—too indifferent, actually, to be called even that. It hurt me more than if it had been a lool of unmasked misanthropy.

'No,' I said, and sat up in bed, pushing the pillows aside. 'No. You know what I really wish to do, Gautama? I should like to go south—to Travancore, Cochin, Mysore, Malabar, all those places.'

'In summer? In the heat? Why?' he asked, surprised.

'I want—I want,' I stammered swiftly,, 'to see the Kathakali dances. I have heard of the ballets they have in their villages. They say they go on for days and days! And the dancers are all men, and they wear such fantastic masks. And the drums. . .'

'Well, well' Gautama was amused. 'I thought I' could never underestimate your appetite for the curious. But I was wrong—I had underestimated it.'

'But, Gautama, I thought you would be interested in that, too—more than in the hills, and pony rides and things. It must be such a—marvellous sight, so—violent, and—bizarre.' I groped for words painfully. The vision was excruciating in its vividness to me, and here

42

was one who did not even glimpse it, no matter what I said. 'The masks they wear—you must have seen them? And their costumes. And the special kind of music. And it is all out in the open, at night, by starlight—and perhaps they have torches. Yes, I suppose they dance by torchlight. . .'

Gautama got up abruptly, having finished his cigarette, and stretched. 'If that is your only reason for wanting to go all that way south, I suggest you wait till a Kathakali troupe comes to give a performance in Delhi, as it is bound to some time—perhaps in winter. It will be less expensive.'

When with my father, even breakfast in the garden—for, on bright winter mornings, we have the servants bring it out into the flower-beds—becomes a party, as good as a revel of elves and fairies who feast on melons and syrups by moonlight. (As a child, I enjoyed, princess-like, a sumptuous fare of the fantasies of the Arabian Nights, the glories and bravado of Indian mythology, long and astounding tales of princes and regal queens, jackals and tigers, and, being my father's daughter, of the lovely English and Irish fairy tales as well, that were read out to me by him, that inveterate reader-aloud, so that a doll dressed in pink I named Rose rather than Gulab, and the guards of Buckingham Palace were nearly as real to me as the uniformed cavalry officers who practised, in a magnificent vertigo of yellow dust, on the *maidan* in the army cantonment where I was sometimes taken for a drive, in the evenings.) My father peels a loquat for me, with a fastidiousness that is a pleasure to watch. 'Can you believe it,' he says, 'that there are

43

people who tuck into smoked fish and liver and kidneys at this time of the day?' and the finely groomed hand that places slivers of fruit upon my plate seems made of alabaster and ivory, fashioned by those magic carvers of ivory that sit beside the Taj Mahal, creating one humble replica of the inamorata's mausoleum after another. 'Ugh.' I say, pulling a face at his words so that he smiles. 'Yes,' he says, 'for so many years I was served lumpy porridge and charred meat at seven in the morning, and, being hungry as a wolf, I had no alternative but to swallow it. But I made a vow then, never to have anything but fruit in the mornings, when I was in a position to order it. I have kept that vow, and I hope you will keep it for me.' Our table is laid beside a mandarin orange tree—there is one in each corner of the garden — a little faery tree, with its glossy leaves, and an overload of small, bright globules of fruit, like miniature lanterns on a carnival night. The servant who stands beside us, and has been with us through the years that his beard grew from a faint haze to the full white fall it is now, says, 'The cook will make orange marmalade today,' and begins to collect the fruit into a bowl. 'Marmalade!' cries my father, raising his napkin to his mouth. 'What a dreadful thought—connected with that lovely tree.' But when I play battledore-and-shuttlecock, using the small bright oranges as shuttlecocks that shoot, bird-like, through the air and are broken, egglike, on the grass he only laughs to see me leap and fly, leap and fly.

It is only from me that he tolerates such things, however. When the woman with loose, straggling hair who has sunk into one of the wicker chairs, sobs 'I must leave him, *Raisahib*, I cannot bear it—I must leave him immediately, if only I could buy a railway ticket. . .' his face grows ascetic, his profile sharpens with distaste, and he places fingertip against fingertip and says, 'Hmmm,' looking over the top of her head at me, with battledore in one hand and three mandarin oranges in the other. When she has been sent away, sniffling, in the large grey car, with all the assistance that he has found it prudent to give the wife of a friend, he says, still looking at me. 'It is remarkable what a magnet human nature can be for disorder and failure. Disorder. I really cannot tolerate it. How can a civilized and highly educated man like Sapru permit a situation to develop wherein all the peace and order of his household disintegrates? It is sheer irresponsibility.' He shakes his head and folds his napkin meticulously. As one neat crisp white square settles upon the other, as one long crease straightens and flows into the next, so do his thoughts, his life, his attitude, his learning and his career assume a similar pattern—formal as a Moghul garden, gracious and exact, where breeding, culture, leisure and comfort have been brought to a nice art, where no single weed is allowed to flower, no single flower to die and remain on the stalk, no single stalk to grow out of its pruned shape. As the streams in a Moghul garden flow musically through channels of carved marble and sandstone, so his thoughts, his life flow, broken into small, exquisite patterns by the carving, played upon by altering nuances of light and shade, but never over stepping their limitations, never breaking their bounds, always moving onwards with the same graceful cadence.

'Why was she wearing a dirty sari?' I ask him, still standing there, clutching my toys. 'She hadn't even done her hair,' I add, with displeasure equal to his, for that crumpled garment, that straggling hair, those hot tears had been something shocking, something unsavoury to me, in the context of this flowering garden, the four mandarin trees, one in each corner, the folded white napkin on the starched white tablecloth. 'She *was* a mess.'

Suddenly my father laughs. It is not a forced laugh as an older man's at a child, but laughter that comes naturally from a life that has as much room for love and for pleasure as for order and discipline. He is delighted that I should have shown a share in his fastidious tastes, amused by my observations. He forgives me the blobs of broken fruit all over the lawn. 'Come, let me see you play,' he says, and waves aside the newspaper that has arrived for him. 'We shall see how high you can toss this orange.'

'No one, no one else', I sobbed into my pillow as Gautama went into the bathroom, 'loves me as my father does.' The curtain fell to behind him, in tragic folds. He did not hear me—the tap was running. The vacuum into which I spoke made me more frantic, and yet he was not really meant to hear. In Gautama's family one did not speak of love, far less of affection. One spoke—they spoke—of discussions in parliament, of cases of bribery and corruption revealed in government, of newspaper editors accused of libel, and the trials that followed, of trade pacts made with countries across the seas, of political treaties with those across the mountains, of distant revolutions, of rice scarcity

46

and grain harvests . . . They had innumerable subjects to speak on, and they spoke incessantly. Sometimes, in order to relax, they played games of cards, so swiftly, so nervously, so intently, that they found they had to release the mounting pressure by conversing, and would begin to talk again, of political scandal and intellectual dissent.

His mother, whose long black hairpins showered down from her hair as profusely and unrestrainedly as black print from a newspaper, and whose armpits were always stained with perspiration, for she moved so much, worked so hard, in passing me by, smiling, said, 'It was wise of Gautama to have married you, Maya,' in a voice at once soft and broken with harshness, so that I could not tell whether she said this out of affection or had some motive far removed from any personal feeling. She looked at me absently, yet smiled warmly, before she rushed away, like some busy rhinoceros charging through the forest, to her dispensary, or her creche, or her workshop for the blind, the disabled, the unemployed. . . She knew so many people, gathered from such diverse backgrounds and situations, that I wondered how I could mean anything more to her than yet another human being to be made comfortable in a hostile world. Yet she paused, and wondered, 'Shall I take you to the dispensary with me?' and shook her head, replying to herself, 'No, it will tire you too much,' before she hurtled down the stairs in the dark passage, towards the tram stop. Or, in the evening when she was home again and had drawn out her account-books with a great clatter, opened them out on her vast lap and begun rapidly to calculate, she looked up to say, 'When will your father send me another cheque, Maya? Tell him I need it urgently—

the nurses in the creche have not been paid this month.' Then she withdrew behind her books, and I knew I was not even one of those human beings whose comfort and health she felt responsible for, but merely one of those outsiders who could be used for this purpose and were therefore necessary, though not necessarily loved. Yet even the pariah pups that she had picked up from the steets would draw close to her feet as though to the most safe and congenial spot they knew of, and there scrabble and drool happily over her battered slippers while she moved her lips silently over the accounts, drew out hairpins with which to scratch her head, and dropped them absently on the ground. The electric bulb over her head had no shade, and it made her, who was as stout as she was short, look gaunt, her face harrowed. Now and then she would look up to say, 'You haven't finished already? Eat more, children. Don't waste anything.' I rarely saw her eat anything herself, though she drank several tumblers of tea each day.

Her childern paid her little attention. There were many of them—two of them students still, the others journalists, teachers, scientists. Gautama the eldest, sat at the table with them, marking lines into the wood with a tin fork as he spoke. They shouted with laughter. He continued to speak, They argued. Was it politics again ? I wondered, conscious of the ache in my arms because I had held my sister-in-law's baby so long. No, not this time. It was a legal case Gautama was defending. It was I who ought to be able to discuss it with him rather than they, I vaguely felt. But they left me out of it with a naturalness I had to accept for they knew I would not understand a matter so involved, and I knew it myself. They spoke to me, the synocete, only when it had to do with babies, meals, shopping, marriages, for I was their toy, their indulgence, not to be taken seriously, and the world I came from was less than that—it was a luxury they considered it a crime to suffer, and so dammed it with dismissal. Restless in my silence, I folded the faded mauve coverlet around the baby's double chin, and wiped a thin line of spittle away from his mouth. His lips were pink and tenuous, exposed and defenceless, like moist, peeled fruit. 'When will he get his teeth ?' I murmured. No one paid attention. The dogs on the floor snarled as they fought over the slippers, and out on the street someone ran shouting. In that stark room, I was the only one who wore a sari of a bright colour. The rest wore colours that no one could care about. But the electric light was very bright. Sometimes the mother looked up and frowned, her forehead furrowed and her lips moved as though in sleep. Her hands were rough and chapped, the knuckles large and knotted.

Their father coursed along routes too swiftly for them to follow. Somewhere, his train rushed crazily through the night, this same night, screaming as it came to the green signal at a remote level crossing and, without slowing, sped on, leaving the small signalman waving a pointless flag, lonely and sad at the door of his whitewashed hut in the middle of the desert that was so cold at night. The train had woken up his dog, and the night was rent in two by its long howl, filled with mourning for the pitiless, bitter world where men found no security, no repose. The man did not like to hear such a howl, and shouted at the dog. But the

49

train had already gone far beyond the sand dunes and was still charging on, carrying away the father who leant his head against the window-pane, so that the neat bones of his skull were being rattled apart. Being tired, he slept, and his sleeping body alone was conscious of the wheels that revolved under him, spinning around at berserk speed, speeding down the long tracks that glittered like lead in the starlight. But his mind was undisturbed by that motion, and at last found sleep, a stationary peace such as his physique had known for so many years, in jail, as a political prisoner while India's independence hung uncertain as an unfurled flag at half-mast. Once he was released, his period of activity had begun, and once he had walked out of his cell, he continued to speed through the nights and days of what was, to him, a new epoch. He was small and frail, almost too slight to bear the weight of his large head. Only when he struggled onto a train and found himself a seat in a third-class compartment, that, out of sheer weariness, did he cease to think of this new epoch—its irritations and failures, its red tape and corruption, its small pale hopes and frustrations and, above all, its great glory, its effect upon the countless villages and cities that he visited— and, as his tired body was flung on to the next stop, his mind returned to the solitary silence of the prison cell, as though martyrdom was its true home. One day he would write a book—when he had time. He dreamt of this book.

A dog began to bark hysterically in the street, and the mother started as though she, too, suddenly remembered the train that had gone berserk in the desert, and saw the signal-man who stood sadly near the green light, and his disconsolate dog. She seemed to shiver, as though she, too, felt the cold. But, seeing me draw the coverlet away from the baby's face, she said, 'It is warm,' as though she were reassuring herself of a fact that had been momentarily obscured by her sharp, brief longing to be with that man, on his journey through the free land, the free night. She returned quickly to her accounts. I walked towards the window, and heard Gautama say 'Certainly not,' and 'It is best to bring it out in the open,' and one brother say 'But faith in the government,' and another 'The opposition's ridicule,' and the unshaded electric bulb burned into the back of my neck. Out in the street, the lamps were dimmer, almost obliterated by the night. The *pan* and soda vendors who, in the daytime, lined the street with their wares, had shrouded themselves in white sheets and lay, corpse-like, on their barrows or across door-steps that spanned open gutters that had at last stopped gurgling. It was very late. The windows of the flats opposite ours gaped like stained gaps of an old man's gums. But there was a moon. A great moon of hot, beaten copper, of molten brass, livid and throbbing like a bloody human organ, a great, full-bosomed woman who had mounted the skies in passion, driven the silly stars away from her, while she pulsed and throbbed, pulsed and glowed across the breathless sky. I spun around, clutching the baby, to stare at my relations, whose names I knew, whose moods I sensed, whose hands I touched, and found there was not one amongst them to whom I could cry, 'Look, look—there is a moon in the sky!'

'I will never go there again,' I swore, flushing again at the memory, 'I will never go there again.' I listened to the tap running, to Gautama gargling, and suddenly the palms of my hands grew moist as it struck me that there might not be time to go there again, even if I wanted to, and I did, desperately. I wanted to race up those filthy stairs to that dismal flat and place a Kashmiri lamp-shade, painted with irises and kingfishers, over the naked bulb, and kiss the mother's hand, and each separate calloused knuckle, and hold the baby in the cradle of my arm, rejoicing in its weight, and listen to the many voices, their gay inflections, their varied tones, their loud, quick rasping over my ear-drums, all those seething human sounds. . .Now, when I surged, open-armed, towards them, all receded to some distant background, and were merely a part of that multitude for which I ardently and futilely longed, to whom I was about to say good-bye, for I might never see them again. In the shadows that spanned the ceiling above my bed, I saw the shadow of the dancer spring to life, and I knew there was no time left, no time left at all.

As always happened to me, it was after my most anguished moments that a piece of truth fell into my exhausted mind—the truth that it was not for them that I longed with fiercest desire, not even for Gautama, but for my gentle father who would have said to me, with that assured and reassuring calm, 'It will all be well, it will all be well soon, Maya.' He had often had to hold me in his arms, or, when I was smaller, wash the tears from my face, and repeat those mesmerizing words to me in his deep tones. As I grew older, the charm was expanded, new phrases were enveloped to give me more room for thought. 'It is best to accept, Maya. What good does it do to cry?' 'Why must you get so upset ? Surely it is all for the best.' 'It cannot be undone now, and it must be accepted as it is—you will find that to be the wisest course.' As I had been a wayward and high-strung child, I heard these phrases frequently, and each time I felt them soothe me like a stream of cold water that tumbled through the ferns of Darjeeling, like the cold, pearl mists that crept over the blue hills and poured into the valley.

I raised my arms over my head, waiting for the memory of those words, that voice, to bring about the desired lull. But it did not come, and I cried, 'I should like so much to see him, Oh, I should like to see father again. It has been so long. . .'

Gautama came out, wiping his hands on a towel. 'What did you say ?' he said, and flung it over his head and began to rub his hair frantically, punishing his ears as well.

I winced at his violence, and my father's hair gleamed soft and white as a bird's wing in mist and shadow. Rather shrilly, I repeated 'I said, I wish I could see father again. It always helps.'

'Helps what ? Whom ?' he asked, puzzled, and flung the towel to the floor where it made a soft, damp plop like a limp dead bird thrown down.

'Help—' I said, and then that too collapsed upon the floor with the towel. Help what ? Whom ? And how ? How to explain ? To warn ? A flock of problems arose, dark birds rising from ominous trees. Without knowing what he had done, Gautama had laid his finger, and forced mine upon the fatal vulnerability of what I had believed in like a fond fool. My father, with his quiet words, would have done nothing to allay my fear or dispel my conviction, but merely underlined

53

their power by asking me, however sadly, to accept, 'for it must be so.' In his words, 'It must be so.' If he saw disaster he saw it as being inevitable, and if he saw rebellion, he saw it as being hopeless. Hence all the tenderness in his voice when he said to me, 'Come now, we mustn't fret. If it must be so, we must learn to accept.' This might have quelled fears of the dark, of bogey men, of unsympathetic school-teachers, but, faced by this great new danger, he would have known of no way of alleviating or dismissing it. He might even, I admitted now, be unwilling to do so, for he was, after all, a fatalist, a born one, and fatalism gave the resignation to his sighs and the gentleness to his voice. Dipping his long fingers in a silver bowl, shaking the drops from the tips like large tears, wiping them dry on a clean cloth, he would nod a little sadly, yet smiling at his dishevelled daughter, and say, 'You will learn one day, Maya, that these things you must put up with. If one can do nothing about them, why not accept?' But how, when it is a question of death? How, father? He did not hear for he was lifting a *pan* out of a small tray, deftly removing the long clove that held the leaf pinned into its tight cone, unobtrusively packing it into his mouth so that the silver foil did not even touch his lips, and, half-closing his eyes, he said, half in a dream, 'The source of disintegration is the human being's vanity in his power to act. Not realizing the futility of his rebellion, he steers himself further and further out of the orbit in which he was born to act, and destroys himself. The world is full of destruction that is born of the Western theory of life, not an Asian one. We have been taught for generations to believe that the merit of accepting one's limitations and acting within them is greater than that of detroying them and trying to act beyond them. One must'—and he dropped his voice—'accept.' In his eyes there appeared a vision of the life he had accepted when he had inherited it, with its luxuries and its responsibilities, its demands and inhibitions. There was nothing but pride, a gentle, well-bred pride, in his manner of acceptance. But when he turned to smile at me, there was all the pain of parenthood upon his lips, chastening and subduing. 'Is that so difficult to see, Maya ?'

And I sprang out of bed so quickly that Gautama raised an eyebrow in surprise, cried, 'Oh no, it wouldn't do at all,' rushing to pick up the cat who had entered by the window, bearing in her liquid eyes the aqueous shade of the shubbery where she had wandered all night, and gathered her fiercely to me, knowing she resented it. Gently she attempted to struggle away, but I would not let her. Bare feet on bare tiles, night-cooled fur against bed-warmed flesh— I was acutely aware of all this, of all that my father would have dismissed with a slow, melancholy smile, waving it away like a lingering drop of water from his fingers, before he turned to his books and papers. 'Leave it,' he would say, seeing the cat struggle, seeing winter draw to an end. 'Let it go—it must be so.'

Gautama had ceased to pay attention, to express surprise. He finished his toilet in silent exasperation, knowing that I stood there, longing for him to question me, so that I could break forth, and holding myself back out of an instinctive dread. I squeezed the cat tightly, and with a little yell of petulance she freed herself and dropped to the floor, shook herself a little but did not rush off like an angry kitten—instead, she stood her ground with dignity, and began licking her tousled fur as though I had sullied it with my hot, grabbing hands. This vexed me farther.

'I won't be going after all,' I said, nearly crying, and the glare from the unshuttered windows stinging my eyes.

'Where?' Slowly, after a long, deliberate pause.

'To Darjeeling—with father.'

'Oh,' he said. 'How was I to know what you meant? You might as well have been referring to that dinner at the Lals next week—I suddenly remembered that.'

'Dinner ? Out ? Next week ?' I cried. 'Oh, I had forgotten,' and, rather put out, I sat down on the bed again, lifting one foot into my hand as I grew calmer and more aware of a world that lay beyond the enclosed one which Gautama and I and, recently, the swart shadow of the pale albino inhabited, and grew steadily less real and less meaningful as the dance within grew more urgent, more significant.

Once upon a time it had been a world peopled with friends as solid as shadows now were to me, and the desire in my fingers to touch and feel them—the grain of their souls and the finish of their personalities—was as strong as though they had been made of poppy petals or silken tapestry, not of skin that is susceptible to dry scales, and hair that is rough and unruly—neither of them nearly as satisfactory to the senses as those finer products of art and nature.

Poppy petals. There was always something about Leila that reminded me of poppies. 'White poppies,' I qualified to her, 'though I have never seen one.

56

Perhaps you make me think of opium, Leila,' and I touched her white wrist slashed with azure veins that plunged to the surface, then disappeared beneath thick swellings. They were always bare—she wore no jewellery. She laughed. 'I like that—considering my day is twice as long as yours, and you've just caught me in the middle of my housework.' Yes, but her actions seemed as detached from her body as her words and her harsh, loud voice from her soul. The only work I ever saw her do that was in keeping with her personality was her ministration to her husband who lay, dying of tuberculosis, upon his still bed in one corner of their single room. He had been dying of tuberculosis when she fell in love with him, and she had married the fatality of his disease as much as the charm of his childish personality or the elegance of his dark hair falling across his white brow. When I saw her hand him a glass of medicine, or lift his body into comfortable positions, I saw in her movements an aching tenderness subdued, by a long sadness, into great beauty and great bitterness.

Today I longed to see her. I even prepared to go out and meet her. Then I recalled that she would not be at home, but in the girls' college where she taught Persian literature to a handful of girls who, while waiting, coyly, for suitable marriages to be arranged for them, read allusions to sly and underhand sex in every romanticism, and yawend at the smallest sophistries. They were a part of the reason for the bitter twist of her mouth and the harsh furrows that ploughed two black lines from the corners of her flaring nostrils to the corners of her lips. It amused her husband to hear her speak of them, however, and she

57

would often do so, revealing what she knew of the smallness of the human mind, its hardness and coarse, obscene resistance to any touch of tenderness, or the wisdom that arises from tenderness. It pained me to hear her speak like this of people with whom she had to spend hours each day, and yet I admitted to her wit and perception, and laughed too, when she read passages from their essays to us, before handing them to her husband to correct. I knew that, later, she would go through the corrections he had made, alter the marks he had ascribed to each essay, but I do not think his vanity allowed him ever to suspect this. Sometimes I thought of him as an animal, a ferocious and wild beast that had allowed itself to become a house pet for its own reasons, and he accepted the food and drink she earned for him, as his due, even teasing her about her parents who had not seen her, written to her, or in any way communicated with her since the day of her elopement. But when I saw her tend him, and the loveliness that entered her closed face as she did so, I could not grudge her what had become the meaning of her life. Leila was one of those who require a cross, cannot walk without one.

But 'Leila', I sometimes raged, 'why don't you ever have fun? I wish you'd come and have tea with me, and then Gautama could take us out. . .' 'I'm in the middle of the examinations, my dear,' she would reply. 'Besides, you cannot imagine what fun it is laying bare the ignorance of my pretty little dunder-heads. Even when they see it spread out and dissected before them, they can't recognize it, poor things.' And the wry, tortured smile that distorted her face. And then, again, she could be so open-hearted, sisterly towards me, begging me to talk of my family and friends, laughing as vividly as only those who laugh seldom can, that I would assure myself of her friendship, her affection for me, and I placed my bare foot on the ground, prepared to leap up and write her a note, telephone her, somehow tune myself onto her especial wave-length of wisdom combined with calm.

I never did achieve this, however, and what halted me was not a remembrance of Leila bitter, but a memory of Leila resigned. Had she raged, revolted, I should have rushed to her now. But even she had ceased, once, to do so. I had gone to see her on a day when I heard her husband had had another attack, and found him lying stupefied with fever, while Leila corrected papers, in a frenzy, at the foot of his bed. She had tea made for us, and I watched her probing fingers ceaselessly twitch and jerk across the tea things, at her clothing, her pencils, like insects in search. She let forth a torrent of hot words and such curses that I sat shocked and silent, prim almost, beside her. But it calmed her to have me there, and after some time her hands grew slack, her body too tired for further movement, and she sank down on the divan, smiled at me out of the shadows of fever, illness and weariness. 'Pay no attention to me today,' she said, softening her hoarse voice deliberately. 'I don't know why I rave.' She lifted one hand to her face, and, with four fingers, touched the centre of her forehead. 'It was all written in my fate long ago,' she said.

I sat back on my bed, clutching my foot again, in the knowledge that I could no longer bear to see Leila and be reminded of this gesture, those words, for now I had a share in her dark vision.

It was natural, after thoughts of Leila, to turn down a line of friends, sift them through my mind, and come to Pom, the pink, plump, pretty Pom who did not speak of fate, who had never been ill, or overworked, or bitter. I smiled to think of Pom prinking before her mirror, tying up her hair in pigtails with enormous ribbons, or twisting flowers into chignons of astonishing intricacy, painting her mouth, the outlines of her black eyes, her finger and her toe-nails. She was never completely satisfied with her appearance, though always very nearly so. 'Do you think this suits me?' she would ask, holding a new silk material of parrot-green against her cheek, and you had no sooner assured her that it was just her colour than she tossed it from her, crying petulantly, 'I am so tired of green. Whenever Kailash buys me a new *sari*, it is always green. I want to try something *new*,' and she would beg me to come shopping with her, and then burrow through the bazaars like an avid rabbit, leaving a chaos of silks and cottons strewn behind her, as well as the cajolings and curses of a dozen frustrated shop-keepers.

It was of her lust for newness, for brightness, colour and gaiety that I thought now, and it made me smile with pleasure. Silly, plump Pom, I thought, as I hurriedly looked through my cupboard for something bright and gay to wear and meet her, and nearly laughed at the recollection of Pom talking so maliciously about her parents-in-law, with whom she lived, and how she complained about this arrangement. 'I am going to make Kailash move out. We did find a flat—did I tell you?—in a new colony. Everything so smart and just A-I, a brand new flat of course. But do you think he listens to me? "What's wrong with living here? It's so cheap Let's save our money",' she mimicked her husband. 'Bah ! Save money for what? To live here like two mice in one small room, not daring to creep out, for fear *they'll* pounce on you, ask you where you're going, when you'll be back, why you aren't wearing the jewellery they gave you. . . Oh!' This comparison of herself with a timid, crouching mouse in a hole was so comical, I had laughed aloud and teased her, about being so well-fed, so sleek a mouse, with so bright a mouse-hole in which to hide from the cats, what with the livid pink counterpane, the pile of glossy fashion magazines, the rows of painted clay birds and fruits that she collected. She did not object to teasing, she was too good-humoured. Logic, tact, diplomacy—nothing mattered to her who chattered so glibly and gaily all the day long, jumping up now and then to bring out a new pair of shoes, a new set of rings to show me, talking with eagerness and animation of anything that was new and bright, and never, never referring to family, tradition, custom, superstition, all that I dreaded now. I was certain she hated such talk as much as I did, even if she had no reason to fear them. Such things simply did not step over the bright enamelled horizon of her painted world, for such things bore shadows, and shadows were alien to her as once, in a similar world, if a richer and more refined one, they had been alien to me, who now constantly looked behind to see where the purple ghost of the albino followed on silk-swathed, oil-softened feet.

I began feverishly to search through the cupboard again, and the saris that hung there, swayed like

61

water, brushed my cheek, rainbow colours collided and melted into each other, and my hands cascaded over soft silks and chiffons as I murmured to myself, 'Lavender? Lilac? Aubergine?' as an invocation to the host of brilliancies that could obscure any gloom. And, by and by, I began to smile again, thinking of the vast lunches Pom could consume, and which her mother-in-law, who had been born in a kitchen and married at its door, would prepare for us when I visited her. How they delighted, this good-humoured, soft-fleshed family, in the riches of Punjabi cooking. Pom's husband would drink *lassi* from a silver tumbler and leave a moustache of white foam upon his upper lip as he sighed, 'Ah-h, how cooling it is,' and then his mother would bring in fresh bread in which pomegranate seeds lay buried, and Pom would search through jars of pickles—tamarind, chilli, lime and venison—for one she particularly craved that day, and all the while the little shining tumblers would be filled and refilled with hot curries and pulses that swam in gravy reddened with spices. With what speed they ate, and what voraciousness, revelling in each flavour, relishing the richness. Afterwards Pom would collapse onto the pink counterpane, groaning. When she fell asleep, of what did she dream? The delicacies that would be provided for tea, the sweetmeats she loved so, the cinema she would be going to thereafter, the drive in the new car. . .

And then I recalled a drive on which she had taken me, and I paused, my hands parting a sheath of peacock blue from one of sea-green. When she had stepped into the car, flaunting her new red heels, I had noticed a bag of sweetmeats she carefully held in one hand, the flowers she clasped in the other—marigold heads and hibiscus petals. 'To Birla Mandir,' she ordered the driver, imperiously, and settled back, arranging the folds of her *dupatta* across her bosom with care.

'Where?' I questioned, not believing my ears. I could not see Pom in the position of prayer and prostration before the idol of Vishnu at the temple, nor could I believe she had honestly considered it.

But yes, 'Birla Mandir,' she repeated briefly, and then her black eyes glinted at me with mischief. 'Couldn't you guess?' she laughed, patting her small, firm paunch. 'I'm to have a baby—in November. I take flowers to the temple every Thursday—I want it to be a boy.'

'But. . .', I said, and 'Pom. . .' and now felt something that had always been strong in me, weaken suddenly and shiver at the memory.

She patted my knee, smiling a suddenly matronly, faraway smile of condescension that pregnant women sometimes have for those not in the same condition. 'I thought you had guessed', she said, 'or that *she* had told you.'

'No', I said, 'no. And Birla Mandir—I never thought you would go there, to pray Did *she* tell you to?'

'Yes. She says I must, if I want a son. I suppose she knows,' Pom mused, crumpling the petals in her hand. 'She has four sons.' Then she smiled. 'Why? Does it seem funny to you that I should listen to my mother-in-law?'

'Yes,' I had replied, 'funny,' and gazed out of the window at the yellow dust through which the car ploughed, and now into the depths of an ocean with its quiet colours.

I ceased to hunt then, ceased to plan, and merely laid my face into those cool cloths, odorous with camphor and lavender, that recalled mountain waters to me, ferns, and nights full of stars, for I found myself alone with them after all. There was not one of my friends who could act as an anchor any more, and to whomsoever I turned for reassurance, betrayed me now. I flung away from the cupboard, setting the silks swaying and swishing, and banged the door shut, wondering whether to hurtle into bed again or fling myself on the floor. But it was all the same. Wherever I laid myself, I could think only of the albino, the magician, his dull, opaque eyes, the hand twitching the fold of cloth between the swallowing thighs. It seemed real, I could recall each detail, and yet—God, Gautama, father, surely it is nothing but an hallucination. Surely not, I sobbed. And once the night of oneirodynia was over, I should be sane again, and in the daylight I should know all this to be nothing but a fulgurant nightmare. Should I not?

3

'It was horrible,' I ground out in rage. 'It was so horrible.' And Gautama, who had undressed, was yawning, was waiting for me to turn out the lights, said, at last, in the cold, calculated voice of one whose impatience is controlled only by weariness, 'What is so horrible *now* ?'

'The whole evening—everything!' I cried, throwing out an arm so that the ruby in the ring that had been a present from my father, fell like a drop of king kite's blood through the air. 'And you thought so too—I could see you were wretched, Gautama, you know you were.'

'Now why on earth should I be wretched because a party, or my host, or the guests did not measure up to my conception of wit or charm? I might have been bored, yes, but, really, wretchedness is a strong word for the normal, everyday mediocrity a man puts up with all his life.'

Not one, but a thousand drops of blood, a thousand ruby-red hammer-heads showered across my vision, blinding me with a fury that might have boiled up within the head, but now exploded before my eyes. 'You were bored? *Bored*? Didn't you feel anything more? Can't you feel anything except boredom? You weren't stifled in that house? You didn't want to weep when you saw that pregnant woman? You were just—bored?'

Having screamed this at him, the red volcano subsided, and I saw I had startled him with an outburst that he had not bargained for. He spoke to me in the cool, styptic tone he employed when wishing to combat my indiscipline with his sense of the practical. 'Frankly,' he said, 'if a man were to react to the sight of pregnancy by bursting into tears, Maya, no court of law would consider him sane or sober.'

'But Gautama,' I insisted, and jumped up to lean over the bedstead so that the fold of my peacock blue, rubystarred sari slid from my·shoulder onto the white pillow, and, by gulping and choking, attempted to control the voice that continued to scream inwardly, 'don't you feel any more than *that*?'

'More than what?'

'More than boredom? More than—than just accepting a fact?'

'Facts are made to be accepted—to be studied. Not to be wept over. Are you changing?'

'Why should I change? I can't sleep now!' I retorted, and fell to biting my lip.

'Well then, your sari is coming undone.'

I tore it from my body and let it sink onto the floor in a whorl of spitting colours, like a flamboyant dancer collapsing through sheer exhaustion, and threw back my head to scream at him. But now he was perturbed at the lengths to which I was carrying this, and said quickly, 'Maya, do sit down. Don't stand there looking like that.'

'Looking like what?' I heard a thin voice shrill, as kites do when they battle in air, and barely recognized it as my own.

'As though you were preparing to plunge off a cliff. I don't even understand what you are working yourself up over. Were you that miserable?'

His voice dropped, the sarcasm was allowed to lie low while concern took over. His words were like an affectionate pet cat's paws running across my taut back. I relaxed then. Like a foolish baby, I sat down upon a pillow and saw, opposite me, a round-faced child in a white petticoat gazing bleakly out of the silvered mirror. Her lips were very red and pouted ridiculously. A posy awry, a tear streaky—it completed the picture that shocked me with the realization that a man like Gautama could hardly be blamed for reacting to it as to a wayward, trying infant, no more.

I bent my head in misery, trying not to cry.

But his voice continued softly. 'You are a grown woman now, Maya, no light-headed child. You must not allow yourself to grow so upset about these things. What if they do live in a grubby house? What if she is pregnant again? What if they were so dull? Why should you allow it to affect you in this manner? There is nothing constructive in your misery, after all. Besides, your life is your own, so different from theirs— your world completely separate. Tell me, is any part of your life as drab, or as depressing as theirs? You must not allow yourself to grow so painfully involved. . .'

Involved. Out of all his flat, equable, grey as steel and leafless words, he would always have one to drop into my ear ominously as a large, round pebble in a still, small lake—a shallow lake, so that it quickly fell to the bottom, and bubbles and ripples rose and spread rapidly. Involved. The crux of the matter—of this disastrous evening that had reduced me to a maudlin child crouching on a pillow and pouting to hold back salt tears. It was all because I had grown too involved. He was so perfectly right. Here lay the catalysis of my unrest. I had grown too involved.

Long black bars at the windows shut us in, and the thin walls of the small room locked us all close together. There was something furtive about our movements, a tenseness in our voices, as though we were performing a scene from a play in the confines of a cage, for the benefit of a heavily breathing though invisible audience. It was strange how impossible was relaxation at a party where most of us were meeting each other for the first time, and therefore had nothing against each other, no aggressive or defensive weapons. And yet they were there—even though we did not call them, admit to them, as weapons. It was as though the end of this party, this evening, was not pleasure at all—but merely information, and in order to gain this, we probed the muddy depths of our neighbours' minds with dull-edged prongs, clumsily, at the same time attempting to air our social graces into the bargain. Perhaps information would ultimately bring about friendliness, ease. . .though I did not really believe this, as I unhappily watched the two ladies beside me, on the sofa.

Mrs. Lal, who had a stye in one eye, was surreptitiously trying to wipe away the orangeade she had slopped onto the table, and caught my eye. 'We have to have burglarproof grilles in all our windows. There are so many thefts.'

'Reely?' said a prim lady in an orange spotted sari, who had a mouth strangely like an ant-eater's snout. 'Near-by?' she asked, and drew her feet together as though to draw away from the rising tide of crime.

'Oh yes,' said Mrs. Lal. 'Every night we hear of a theft in some house or the other.'

'Oh,' said the prim lady, wiping her astounding snout with a little lace-edged handkerchief. 'You must be very frightend at night.'

'Oh yes,' said Mrs. Lal, nodding desperately, and bumped into another half-full glass of orangeade in her attempt at mopping up. She jerked her head back and cast a nervous glance at her husband. 'At night I am always so frightened, I can't sleep,' she confessed.

The prim lady then turned to me. Her eyes were perfect circles, their edges darkened with kohl that glistened. 'And do you have many thefts in the Civil Lines?' she enquired. We had already discovered each other's addresses, plus various other credentials.

'No,' I said, 'I don't think I have heard of any.'

There was a dull pause. The hostess's eyes glazed with desperation. Gulping, she turned to the prim lady and asked, 'Do you have many thefts where you stay?'

The gentlemen burst out laughing. 'Oo-ho-ho-ho,' they roared in unison—Gautama slightly out of tune —and plump Mr. Lal wiped tears from his eyes before he hurried to refill their glasses with whisky from half a bottle. The prim lady's husband, a large Sikh in a tight suit and a pink turban that was slightly awry, looked over his shoulder to see if any of the ladies had heard, then turned his back to continue the joke.

A ghastly hush gripped the ladies. We picked up our glasses all at once, we all sipped together. If we had ever had the capacity to live with silence, it deserted us now, and we breathed heavily. A nervous tic seized the corner of Mrs. Lal's mouth. Quickly I began to fabricate a gory tale of theft and murder in our quiet tree-lined Civil Lines with its bunga-lows of dignified, if decaying, respectability. Mrs. Lal shrilled with relieved laughter, with grateful exclama-tions, so that even the men glanced at us. Triumphantly I tried to catch Gautama's eye, but he was staring at his glass, taciturn and strained. At the sound of all this unusual jocularity, the door at the far end of the room opened, and the Lals' small son came trailing in, his face blurred with moist, perspiring sleep, and his eyes brilliant. He whimpered softly and came, crab-wise, to his mother. She, barely noticing the child had crept out of bed to come to her, said to him absently, 'Go and play.' It was past ten o' clock. He anchored himself to the edge of her sari, gnawing at it so that a large, damp stain spread over a corner of it, and watched us with a perplexed, shifting gaze, as though we were figures out of his dreams—stifling, grey dreams in which figures stood speechless in the horror of ultimate realization, incapable of motion or release. An indescribable air of futility had entered the room with the child. It seemed to me that we alone existed upon an island in a city of dead, and that we, too, were gripped by a fatal disease and would soon, slowly, perish since even the youngest, freshest generation was touched by it and had no hope of survival. I stretched out my hand, tried to touch that white cheek. He flung himself back in terror. I made myself smile, speak to him—of what? Of the china animals in the little glass cupboard into which all the ornaments in the room were crammed—dyed rushes in glass jars, glass toys of minute size, dolls in dusty, faded finery, even an Easter egg, mummified. He stared at them, at me, with glazed, unseeing eyes.

'We must have woken him up out of his sleep,' I said, leaving him to himself at last.

'Have you no *ayah*?' asked the orange spotted lady, sipping orangeade.

A purple flush suffused Mrs. Lal's face and neck. She stammered a little, glancing at her husband. 'She —does not stay here at night,' she said, and I longed to slap her, to shake the weakness and falsity out of her uncontrolled face, so that she might speak the truth with peace of mind, even if humour lay forever beyond her reach. 'The—older children look after him very well,' she said, for she had sensed my hard stare.

'You have other children? Sons?'

'No. Four daughters.'

This ought not to have distressed me. I ought to have been able to rejoice at this, as my father had rejoiced in me, saying that in a daughter he had a treasure. Yet now the word brought up visions of dowries, of debts, humiliations to be suffered, and burdens so gross, so painful that the whole family suffered from them. Why? I was angry with myself, yet could not shake off the truth, and when the prim lady clucked her tongue in sympathy, I said nothing.

The boy trailed after us into the dining-room when dinner was announced by a ragged urchin in coal-dusted striped pyjamas, who looked as though he too, had been woken from exhausted sleep, in a coal-bin. The table had evidently been laid by him—the griminess and the finger-prints on the plates confirmed this. The vegetables were all colourless and slimy, the rice was cold and lumpy. Mrs. Lal scarcely dared serve us. From the open door to the bedroom, a swaddle of tired, patched mosquito nets was visible. The bodies of the four sleeping girls, who lay under them, tossed and sighed and groaned. The electric fan revolved noisily over their heads, a grotesque, bat-like piece of machinery, evil and threatening.

'You have no air-conditioner?' the prim lady asked Mrs. Lal, in a tone cold and amused and hateful.

This brought Mrs. Lal to the end of her tether. Giving a nervous jerk, she swung into her pot-bellied husband, knocking aside his plate piled high with

71

rice and pickles, and hit her forehead against his jutting chin. She was helped upright amidst much masculine laughter and feminine giggling, and she stood there, awkwardly jabbing at two large yellow curry stains on the front of her sari.

'And such a pretty sari,' lamented the orange-spotted lady, having little taste.

The husband took it as an excuse to load his plate still higher. Mrs. Lal dared not look at him. She had obviously hurt her head, or perhaps her eye, for she rubbed it furiously, till it was red and weeping.

'Oh-ho-ho! Accident! Accident!' boomed the Sikh, his even rows of teeth gleaming as he laughed heartily.

'Have you hurt yourself?' I asked her at last, for she seemed unable to recover what poise she might once have had.

'No,' she said, with surprising decisiveness, and the line of her lips plunged downwards in a queer, hard grimace of unutterable bitterness. 'That was the accidental part of it,' she said, and I saw, from the swell of her stained, limp clothes, that she was pregnant.

My hand lay soft and plump and tender, on the glitter of peacock blue silk, one finger rather swollen and pink because the ruby ring was a little tight. It looked like a warm, well-fed pigeon brought to earth—or sea—by a bullet, its tiny wound open and bleeding. I turned it over and gazed at the palm, which was so pink from having been pressed to its partner so long, that the lines were hazy and indistinct.

'What a tyrant he is,' I sighed.

72

'Who—Lal? Yes, he seems rather a loudmouth—a very shrewd businessman, though,' Gautama said, patiently prepared to gossip with me for an half-hour till I was calm enough to sleep.

But a restlessness boiled within me still. I tried to read the lines on my palm, I fiddled with the ruby, I yawned. 'There were orchids—in a basket on the verandah. Did you see them, Gautama? I wonder where they got them from. They were the kind you find on trees, in Darjeeling.'

'Well, that at least must have been a bright spot in the depressing evening,' he said, smiling a little, slowly and indulgently.

'But Mrs. Lal said they never flower. They are hill orchids, you see. They will soon be dead'.

He started to laugh. 'So it was one long stretch of unrelieved gloom! Poor, poor Maya. And I thought I was doing you a favour by taking you out one evening. I hardly ever do these days.'

I moved towards him to press his hand and reassure him of my gratitude for his gallant attempt. But this evening his sympathy and indulgence failed to arouse in me the usual passion of delight and excitement. The events of the evening, its atmosphere, oppressed me till I felt exanimate. Like a nightmare, it haunted my waking, and I knew I should not be able to sleep at all. Another recollection sailed up and made me sigh. 'And the cabaret—oh, Gautama, that ghastly, ghastly cabaret. I *wish* we had not let the Singhs take us out after dinner.'

His pink turban awry, the large Sikh leant over to place an arm across Gautama's shoulder, in an absurd posture, the more ridiculous for the disparity

between the gaunt, sarcastically silent intellectual
and the prosperous, buoyant, witless fool. Beaming,
he turned to me, who had cringed at this sight,
squirming with the embarrassment I knew Gautama
to feel, and said, 'He never told you that we were
neighbours in the hostel at college? And how I used
to sing so loudly that he would come to the door
to shout at me—or send me a note?'

'No,' I said, and looked away from Gautama whose
face was gashed, momentarily, by a painful smile
of pity.

'No ?' bellowed the Sikh, slapping Gautama heartily on the back. 'Oh-ho, but we used to have good
times, my friends and I. We were always begging him
to come with us to the coffee-house, to look at the girls
from the women's college—oh-ho-ho. Or to come out
and have a good dinner with us—we used to get sick
on that hostel food.'

'And did he ?' I asked, and could not help smiling
myself as I thought of Gautama as a student. Gautama
was thoughtfully filling his glass with ice, his face taut
with the strain of bearing with the irrepressible Sikh,
who continued blithely. 'Never,' he roared. 'He was
always the brainy type. He was always studying, always standing first in examinations. Not like me—who
came last in my class ! Oh-ho-ho-ho,' he bellowed, and
winked at his wife who screwed her ant-eating mouth
into a small red pimple of disapproval at this revelation. 'And after that, I heard what a brilliant lawyer
he has become, and I used to think that I must try and
meet him. But it was not written in our fate to meet
again, till to night.'

The ice-cube that had sunk midway into the murky

amber liquid in Gautama's glass, bobbed up again, and there was a soft, fizzing sound, like a miniature volcano that, after subsiding into an equivocal silence, once more explodes and froths. Fate. The word that had not come to my ears in spoken form, for so long. Banned from our household, banned by my father. Born of a family of Brahmins that for generations had lived their lives—the eating, studying, travelling and marrying that formed the basic structures of their more or less idle lives—according to prescribed patterns, had married according to the advice and suitability of their horoscopes, had diligently taken up careers that the pundits had chosen for them out of the constellations, had had their children's stars studied and speculated upon before they even spoke their first recognizable words. . .my father had thrust them all into the fire together with an unsavoury scrap of paper seized from the *ayah's* hand. From that day, the word had not been uttered in my presence, nor 'astrology' nor 'palmistry'. 'Hush,' he had cried if any such matter were mentioned, and it was with fear that his command was uttered, and with fear that he had watched the little bits of paper, marked with fine Sanskrit calligraphy and strange hieroglyphics, catch fire, curl up at the edges and turn to carbon-black ash. That had been the end of an episode, and I had thereafter forgotten it, played happily, believed the stars to be so many fireflies. Nor had it returned to the orbit of my being with marriage, for to Gautama, no Brahmin and no traditionalist, it was a word alien from birth. Sitting at the uncovered table under the naked electric bulb, how he and his brothers and sisters would hoot with derision at the mention of

75

superstition, with pity and scorn for those who allowed their lives to be ruled by them, and ruined by them. Even his mother would look up from her papers, join in the laughter and, pulling a face, comment, 'What foolishness !' His gentle, almost speechless father might, at the most, smiling, say, 'Fate ? What is that ? I don't know of it—only of work.' Recently I had hesitantly, fearingly attempted to take up the topic with Gautama, but he had disdained to discuss so puerile a subject, and dismissed it by saying, 'Palmistry ? Astrology ? What new fad is your sudden interest in them ? Must we be so childish ? After all, we have both been educated fairly thoroughly, however different the methods,' and then he had held forth on education, for such a topic was permissible, being 'civilised'.

But now—Fate—the word dropped into our midst, burningly mnemonic, subtle as a soundless ice-cube, overwhelming as lava. The wild, irresponsible longing to question, to determine, sang through me and I was swept away by its tide. I leant forward, pressing my finger tips upon the table-top, marking white oblongs of dim moisture on the glass.

But Gautama was ahead of me. He laughed suddenly. 'Now I remember,' he said. 'You were the palmist. You used to sit at a table in the coffee-house and read palms.'

'True ! True !' bellowed the Sikh, thumping him enthusiastically on the back.

My palms began to sweat. Secretly. For I hid them in my lap, curling my fingers across them so that no one should see, no one should know. Softly, softly, I murmured. Here's danger. And yet my blood boiled in the shells of my ears, hammered there. If I did not

76

say something to release the pressure, it would burst as through an overtaxed dam. I turned to the prim lady. 'Do you, too, believe in palmistry ?' I asked her, and my voice broke the words into hard splintered shells of sound that crackled, grated amidst all the clamour of the night-time restaurant.

'Palmistry I know nothing of—nor does my husband, he only pretends,' she snapped, and ignored his indignant spluttering. 'But the stars—I believe in the stars. It was written in my destiny, one astrologer told me, that I was to marry a man from west of the Jhelum, and I did, and that I was to bear two sons, and I did.' Her pointed pink tongue slipped out to lick a drop of coffee off her short lip. Then it withdrew.

Excited, I turned now to the husband who was still protesting at the accusation of pretence. 'And you ?' I questioned. 'You believe in palmistry ? Have you found the lines in your hand dictating *your* life ? You are convinced?' It was important to know, urgent even. It was as though I had now to gather forces to me, before I entered the battlefield. Looking up and blinking at the amber lights and the white shirt-fronts at the tables around me, the flashes of jewellery and the gashes of paint, it seemed to me that out of them I had to pick those who would support me, and that amongst them lurked many who were my enemies. I watched them, avidly. I watched the Sikh's face, searched for the truth even on that shining glaze of well-being, that blank, round openness of childish innocence that became, in this great bulk of a man, ignorance. But the ignorant often know, by instinct, I felt.

He laughed jovially. So jovially that an alliance with the albino of the black and oilslick temple gate was discounted immediately. 'You see,' he said, 'how interested women always become in this! As soon as I mention I am a palmist—even if I add that I am only an amateur palmist—they gather around me like bees. Shall I read your palm then, and tell you your future?'

He reached out his hand, square, hairy, grasping, to receive mine and my destiny. 'No,' I cried, shrinking back. 'Oh no—that is not what I want at all —please.'

'She is afraid you might prophesy bad luck,' said Gautama, and tried to comfort me, in my only too obvious discomfort, with a rare smile. But it travelled to me across so vast a space, climbing across so many traps and pitfalls, that it was rendered pale and cold by the time it came to me. What had boiled within me so lividly, now froze.

'He is making fun of you,' said the Sikh. 'He always was a disbeliever. How often have I proved to him that my prophecies are correct—but he would never listen. Do you know, I prophesied that he would stand first in the B.A. examination?'

'And he did,' I murmured, hypnotized.

'The professors, too, prophesied that, Harbans, if you remember,' said Gautama, drily, with the dispassionate objectivism that divorced pride from any such statement. 'In fact, they were the ones to tell you that, in advance, and you relayed their prediction to me. Right?'

'See?' shouted Mr. Singh. 'The heretic still! Did I not tell you also that you would one day be a great lawyer?'

'How long do you give that prophecy to come

true ?' said Gautama, growing irritated now.

'Let me ask your wife. I can see that *she* believes me.'

'No !' I cried, and stared at Gautama for help. Out of that pit swarming with fellow beings, I had not found one who would help. He alone was my rock in the wild sea—calm, immobile. But now he too turned to me with an expression that displayed surprise at my vehemence, the distraught tenseness on my face. 'I don't,' I insisted, stammering. 'I mean—I don't know. I really don't know—I have to find out.'

'There ! shouted the Sikh. 'She is ready to listen— I will convince her within five minutes—just you watch!'

'No,' I repeated, more insistently, more loudly, for I knew danger was close now, very close, and the Sikh was no ally of mine, but of that magician of the underworld, the albino, his shadow. 'I—I have to find out.'

'What *can* you find out ?' said Gautama, fastidiously destroying a cigarette in a steaming bowl of water. 'No educated adult can seriously be expected to believe that the patterns or the movements of the astral bodies—solids, after all, of earth and ice and rock— or the lines formed in the palms of your hands, and in those of monkeys and gorillas as well, have the remotest influence upon our deeds and actions in our everyday lives—or those of the apes. Can you—seriously ?' he asked me.

'Apes !' cried the Sikh in delight. 'Apes and monkeys ! Oh, the man is a joker, a real joker, isn't he, Manju ? Who is talking of apes ? They only know how to eat and how to mate. No horoscope is needed for that. But our lives are more complicated. . .'

'Are they, Harbans ? murmured Gautama pointedly, in a tone that would have destoyed me.

But the man continued unabashed. 'Sometimes it helps to have a little guidance. Especially women— they are less adventurous than us, and they like to know in advance, and prepare for it. Now is that true or isn't it ?'

Once more he turned to me, and this time I detected in his leer something of the lascivious evil in the smiles and gestures of the albino astrologer, and I perspired freely in panic. 'I don't know,' I cried loudly, defensively. 'How can I tell ?'

'But you believe in fate, don't you ? Don't you ?'

The voice echoed down a tunnel of memory to me, and that one word set playing again the mysterious leitmotive that this year's spring had so disturbingly brought to life. I opened my mouth to scream, in order to bring to a halt that force that had been set so subtly into motion and was driving me to an extreme of insane fear. But just then the band borke into a fast, frolicsome tune, and Mr. Singh's face lit up as he clapped his hands, and cried happily, 'The cabaret ! The cabaret !'

After the rustle, there was a hush amongst the diners, the drinkers and the dancers, now an attentive audience, as the rainbow lights, in a ring around the band-stand, changed silkily from amber and violet to the pink and green of syrupy sweetmeats, sending shimmering knives of light cutting through the glass-topped dance-floor. The drummer—a Goan in a dinner-jacket —beat a warning tattoo upon his drums, and his teeth flashed white in a dark, simian face. One or two of the more excitable onlookers began to clap with the irresponsibility of children, and the prim lady unexpectedly nudged me in the ribs, sharply, with a wicked elbow, and whispered, 'Now look, now look,' with an eagerness I should not have believed her capable of. Then the cabaret began as row of girls of even height came prancing out with a smart tattoo of their wild, hard-hitting scarlet heels.

'Ha-ha,' cried the Sikh, sitting up and setting his turban at a jaunty angle.

With smiles that had been brilliantly painted onto their sallow faces—the colours of many races, Indian Chinese, English, Nordic, Polynesian, running together till each was rendered equally flat, equally compromising—and their large, strained mouths stiff beneath the paint, the dancers went through their routine so leadenly that they even stamped the music out into a kind of quick goose-step march that rang of prison parade-grounds and jailors' beats. They might have been tiredly going through the callisthenics that a necessity for correcting and improving their merchandise—their figures—inflicted upon them, in the privacy of dank, small rooms that smelt of unclean latrines and panting beasts, hidden away in the unlit lanes from which they emerged, nightly, to don the glittering garb of their strenuous trade. The only spontaneous, uncalculated movement to be seen about them was the up-and-down flopping of their loose hair—yellow, orange, red and khaki tints that had been poured out of labelled bottles into wash-basins lined with grease, if not from their widely-travelled ancestors. Vigorously they pumped their long, muscled legs into the air, and soon they began to pant with the effort. Their arms they held in positions martialled into them by unimaginative teachers, but limply, as though they were not conscious that they had arms. The only portion of their anatomies of which two or three, at least, appeared conscious, were their protruberent posteriors, and of which they made much, arousing chuckles of delight amidst our friends who were excited by the very reflection of the girls' spangles that nudged their cheeks and their shirt-fronts.

'Jolly good!' shouted the Sikh, his eyes gleaming at a tall, well-rounded woman of doubtful ancestry—did her lank, fair hair speak of the fjords along the North Sea, or the sharpness of her nose recall a Semite from a brawling city in the Middle East ?—who smiled as she grew aware of his eyes riveted upon her, and now and then made a curious, bouncing movement that made her bosom more prominent, especially for his benefit and of those whose bluish pupils flashed in the underlit pool of smoke beyond, in sly, leering approval. Her smile was weird—the corners of her lips would plunge downwards instead of up, and then she would throw back her arms and head, so that more and more of that white, tallow-like flesh would rear out of her blouse. The music grew livelier, and she began to gyrate wildly in the centre of a ring formed by the others, some kind of macabre, meretricious abandon entering into her movements as though she were shouting, or wanting to shout, 'See what I have ? Like it ? Take it, gentleman, take it, it's yours !' The other dancers plodded around her, growing more leaden and more surely as she grew more careless and flamboyant, for she was, without a doubt, the cleverest of them all. Without any apparent climax, the number came to an end, and the drum beat drooped downwards into silence. The applause was wild, and the anachronistic chandeliers over our heads gently, sadly shivered as the dancers pranced out, the tall woman seeing to it that she dropped a little spangle on the floor which she had to pick up, with a little, provocative upthrust of her rump, and so she was the last to depart and had the most applause to herself.

Again and again they returned, for another and yet another number, and one dance seemed exactly like the other, except that the costumes grew saucier and saucier. Once they came out wearing little paper sailor hats which they threw into the audience with wild catcalls that tingled down our spines as though they were the howls of preying wolves hunting, in packs, in the darkening jungles. A fat man at a table next to ours managed to catch one of the little hats. He clasped it to his bosom and burst into tears of joy. The Management edged towards him.

The popular one, the fair one, had an act to herself then, with a consumptive, redhaired girl to help her. It turned out that she was a contortionist, and she went through a performance as revolting as it was remarkable. This body, that had once lain on grass, on park benches, twined itself round swing ropes and moved through lanes of sunshine and clear rain, and was now her business, her chief merchandise in a market where there was stiff competition, was transformed now into something inhuman—a mass of soft, pulpy tallow that could grow taut, grow rotund, grow angular, could spring out in certain places at a time, lie flat in others, assume postures that shrieked of unnaturalness, toss and twist, fling itself once this way, once that, and all for a hundred fish-eyes that slithered over it, feeling it with quivering antennae, sliding along

83

it as slowly as snails that dribbled white slime over the white flesh. While her set face with its sharp eyes and trembling nose, gave away her intentness on the problems of this contortion or that, and the terrible necessity of avoiding a mistake, a fall, the various parts of her torso appeared to live a mobile life of their own. As she slowly, painstakingly bent her head back so that her hands touched the floor, and she could turn over backwards, her bosom swelled and stood out on display. 'This is my bosom,' a flagrant label read. 'And these are my legs,' proclaimed a second, as she stood on her head and lit herself a cigarette with her feet, while her legs writhed and kicked and waved provocatively. In between these antics, she pranced to little dance tunes, perspiring and panting to get back her breath, and her symmetrically rounded, pneumatic posterior bore its own inviting label. 'Here is my bottom—pinch it!' At the end of the performance, to applause and music, she turned a cart-wheel and winked enormously. 'Liked it?' asked the wink. 'Help yourself!' answered the smile. Grinnig, with the acrobat's relief at having an act safely behind her, she swung past our table, and I saw the perspiration that stood out on her face. Our companion, who noticed no such thing, made a futile grab at the wide, swaying hips and cried, 'Oh-ho, oh-ho!' His wife was smiling tautly at the dancer.

As Gautama had turned out to be, after all, the closest to an ally, now he alone turned to me with an understanding that was shot with concern. 'Maya,' I heard him say, but just then the entire corps came rushing out in a flood of lurid magenta light, to brassy loud music, for the finale. They carried little silver-topped canes which they waved in the air and pointed at men, uttering little animal cries of voluptuous invitation, as cats do when they mate. On their costumes of black net, they wore bright spangles, and each spangle was a price tag, each price tag proclaimed the price of their breasts, their rumps, their legs. The spangles were bright, the prices were low.

When they had made their final departure, the restaurant began abruptly to empty, and there was something bleak and unwelcoming in the flood of normal yellow light that replaced the subtle, hot, suggestive tints that had washed us during the floor-show. In the general din of leave-taking, we could hear the fat man at the neighbouring table sobbing. 'Beautiful! B-beautiful b-bitch!' as he clutched a very rumpled paper sailor hat to him.

'Oh, we should have brought you here last week,' said our companion, as he beckoned to the waiter to refill his glass for he had not had enough yet. 'Last week there was a strip-tease!'

'What! What!' screamed his wife, from whom all primness had departed. Even her ant-eating mouth had widened and loosened. She nudged me again, sharply and crudely and in her laughter there was an underhand vulgarity that condoned a similar quality in the cabaret girls.

Before the lights dimmed to signal time for closing-down, somebody lit the spotlight over the dance-floor, and slid it slowly over the audience like an ironic sneer, unbearably prolonged, and, in catching and illuminating shadowed eyes, rings that caused thick fingers to bulge, teeth that gleamed animal-like, squirms and gestures betraying pleasurable and covert

85

discomfort, it revealed in its banal glow such a seething mass of pimps and lechers, of touts and prostitutes, masquerading in the garments of those who imagine they can afford an attitude of superiority over the poor and the beasts, that I felt myself trapped at an oneiric ball where the black masks that I had imagined to be made of paper turned out to be of living flesh, and the living flesh was only a mockery, a gathering of crackling paper. It was perverse, it was wrong, but it was a fact, a fact that had been taken for the truth. Values were distorted in that macabre half-light with its altering tints, at an hour when those values would have been all-important. What was true? What was lasting? What to believe in? What reject? Danger, danger. . .the warning came whispering over a vast distance to me, struggling through the mass of truths and lies in nightmarish disguise. 'I have to go,' I cried, rising to my feet, and then, more urgently, 'Gautama, I must go.'

The bear balances on its tired feet, his snout up in the air, as though in prayer, and his unexpectedly small frail paws curled, like a sleeping child's, over his once handsome chest where a white horseshoe mark stands out amidst the russet-tinted dark hair. Shaggy, clumsy, old and exhausted, he stands there, waiting, while I and the gardener's five children jump up and down on the grass in delight, gathering up handfuls of turf and scattering it in the lustrous, mother-of-pearl winter morning air, in gross imitation of the bear. The trainer, holding onto a string which is attached to a metal ring that passes through the bear's nose, goes around with his filthy turban turned inside out, singing a song for pity and *baksheesh*. And all the while the bear stands there, his quivering, dew-touched snout lifted into the air which is scented with carnations and oranges— enjoying an interval of memory refreshed between the agony of the brawling asphalt streets, the overfull stalls and thick oil fumes of the bazaars—and he closes his eyes because he cannot bear to see the flat, flat lawn, the white, white house, the many, many people, when his heart is pounding with renewed passion for the wilderness of rain scented firs and the tangled undergrowth of the Himalayan mountains that mark, in the north, a jagged line of azure blue amidst coils of silver mist and the first snowflakes of a long, quiet winter.

I gaze at this magnificent beast from whose thick coat the gloss has sunk into dust, from whose tenebrous eyes all pride and power have gone, leaving only an intent determination to remain tearless. I put my hands to my mouth, then turn and run back into the house where I know there to be a bowl of ripe fruit gleaming on the polished teakwood of the buffet. Bearing two golden bananas in each hand— more I cannot hold—I come rushing out again, race up to the bear, then stop short, for he is so wondrously large, so powerfully dark, standing there on his hind-legs in an attitude of mourning. Then, timorously, I extend my offering. Gently, the bear drops on all four feet, and comes eagerly forward to take it from my hand. Transformed into an overgrown toy through lavish delight, he settles down to strip the bananas, neatly and deftly, and swallow them quickly, quickly.

The gardener's children, who are permitted a great quantity of guavas and oranges, bananas and mangoes from the garden, clap their hands with glee and turn somersaults in ecstasy. But the trainer's face grows clouded. Looking up at him, I see that he is furious, and am a little shaken in my pride at having made the Himalayan beast happy. Yet, when he speaks, he betrays none of the anger that has whitened the taut line of muscles along his jaw. He drops his stentorian voice to a maudlin whine, and cries, 'You have given the beast food, missahib, and not to a poor human being If he is hungry, do I not starve? If he dances for his living, do I not sweat? Alas for the ignorance of the blessed rich! They will not consider a man's hunger any more. Alas. . .' and rolling up his shirt, he begins to rub his belly and moan.

The shrill-voiced gardener's children scream abuse at him, reminding him that he has already been paid, and handsomely too. The trainer turns upon them with fury, returning their filthy words with vehemence. The smaller of them begin to howl. While they are still in the midst of this sudden, violent broil, I run back to the house, seize another armload of bananas, return, perspiring, and hand them to him, my face hot and crimson with shame.

'I was sure,' I explain to my father, when unable to sleep that night, 'that the bear doesn't get much out of his earnings. I'm *sure* he doesn't.'

'Undoubtedly not. It must be the first time the poor fellow got any fruit to eat since he was trapped in the hills,' my father soothes me. 'How he must rub his tummy and smack his lips when he thinks of the apples and pears and strawberries he used to find in the jungles when he was young and free. And perhaps he remembers the honey-comb he found once in an old dead tree, and how he and all his brothers and sisters gorged themeselves on it. Did you know that bears love honey? I must tell you a story about a particular little bear...'

Around this pretty tale he builds for me, he hopes to compose my dreams for the night, for it is the doctor's orders that I must be permitted no anxieties, no excitements. Yet, once I fall asleep, the dream dissolves quickly into a nightmare, in which a row of soft, shaggy, frailfooted bears shamble through a dance routine to the dry rattle of the trainer's tambourine. Then suddenly, behind the bears, an entire row of trainers rise up and begin to dance too, with greater vigour. They kick up their legs, displaying cleft feet, grin hugely and roll up their clothes and rub their bellies and bay at the moon. By a grotesque trasformation, the bears are rendered into a lonely, hounded herd of gentle, thoughtful visitors from a forgotten mountain land, and the gibbering, cavorting human beings are seen as monsters from some prehistoric age, gabbling and gesticulating, pointing at their genitals, turning their backs and raising their tails, with stark madness in their faces...

The doctor has to be called, finally, to give me a little morphine so that I might sleep in peace, and, by my father's orders, no more performing animals are allowed in at our gate.

(Yes, now that I go over it in my mind, my childhood was one in which much was excluded, which grew steadily more restricted, unnatural even, and in which I lived as a toy princess in a toy world. But it was a prety one.)

'Exhibitionism,' said Gautama. 'Nothing but a penchant for exhibitionism. As common a disease as

89

egoism, or megalomania, not to be suppressed.'

'Do you think so? I don't know,' I mused upon my pillow, turning and turning the ring upon my finger, a flower in my hair. 'None of them looked as though they were doing what they wanted to do. They all looked so sad to me—so terribly sad.'

'Hardly sad. Merely vapid.'

'Because they were so unhappy,' I insisted.

'One does not necessarily lead to the other—not to a person of intelligence and discretion.'

'Is it lack of intelligence, do you think, Gautama? I am so afraid they have been thrust into it by evil uncles, or stepmothers—like female children in Japan who are turned into prostitutes by their own families, to earn a living for them all.'

'Come, now, we are going too far. They are merely physically aberrant women of small ambition, who think it a compliment if men leer at their thighs. That only proves to you their level of intelligence. It is sheer pusillanimity that makes them take up this common form of half-way prostitution—the tantalus variety of prostitution, you might call it—and they're as happy as they are capable of being happy. None of them appear contented, I grant. Exhibitionists never can be, there is never enough to exhibit, as there never is enough pleasure to satisfy the jaded. Are you coming to bed?'

'Yes,' I sighed. 'I suppose so,' and got up to fold my sari, length by length. 'But they make *me* sad,' I pursued.

'Poor Maya,' Gautama yawned, half-asleep. 'It has been a depressing evening for you, hasn't it.'

'You see,' I said, dropping the sari and clasping my hands in eagerness to communicate with him, unfold, at last, completely all before Gautama who, being sleepy, might so easily miss the point. 'It is because they are so engrossed in—in all that's gross and *useless*, that they don't see what really matters. All the *truth* in living just passes them by, and I am so sorry for anyone—' yes, even you, unsuspecting husband—'who misses it. It is like spending seventy years of one's life in a graveyard—being born in one, and dying in one. It's a waste—a waste. And one life-time is so short, it's over before you know it!' My voice rose again to a dangerous pitch.

'And what,' he said, smiling, unsuspecting still, 'would you tell them is the truth of living ?'.

His smile was indulgent, even if strained with tiredness, but to me, unsmiling, it was the barrier, the limbo that had always held us separate. Looking down at his thin face, grey and drawn upon the white pillow, it seemed to me that I was climbing a mountain from the top of which could be seen the entire world, unfolded like a map, with sun-silkened trees and milk-mild rivers and jewelled townships amidst fields of grain and valleys and tracts, all fruitful, all florescent, while he, because he did not care for walks, or views, was tired from reading too much, and had matters to think out within the confines of his brain, remained behind in the dusty, enclosed cup of the small plain down below. Were I to force him to follow me, he would follow unseeing. Oh, unprivileged to miss the curved arc of a bird's wing as it forces itself against the weight of air into the clear sky where it can skim the currents with singing ease; the steam rising from a pot of tea, flavoured with orange; the revelation within the caress of a familiar hand, tender, heart-torn, and the speechlessness that goes with it; the persistent, sweet odour of a ripe pineapple, freshly sliced, its pale juice and streaked flesh, pungent and sweet, inhaled with a delight that swells to the point of exploding or of soaring away into the sky; the pages of an exquisite, handbound book, odorous of rice and ripe age, marked with the fine letters suited to the verses inscribed there; phrases of music, lines of verse, cleaving together in the rich all-embracing voice of a baritone drunk with wine; and the untrained voice, as great, as memorable, that rings out on the open road at night, and sets trembling those who hear it while lying sleepless in the moonlight that floods in through open windows; moonlight, its quality and coolness, playing upon papaya leaves, its silver glint cutting sharp, black silhouettes out of those great, marvellously designed leaves; and then the papaya tree in itself...I contemplated that, smiling with pleasure at the thought of those long streamers of bridal flowers that flow out of the core of the female papaya tree and twine about her slim trunk, and the firm, wax-petalled blossoms that leap directly out of the solid trunk of the male. ..

'You can't?' interrupted Gautama. 'Well, I'll let it pass, since it's late, and you looked pleased enough, just thinking of a reply. Come, Maya, I'm half-asleep.'

I looked down at him, and was not annoyed at the interruption, or his yawns, for even they were part of the vivid, explosive, mobile life that I rejoiced in—the world of sounds, senses, movements, odours, colours, tunes. Besides, if I could pleasure in contemplation of the male papaya, how much more food for delight in this male companion, surely. And I melted with tenderness, my arms curled into an instinctive cradle, a possessive embrace, as I went over thoughts of him leaving his clothes on the floor because he never had a thought to spare for such matters, nor time, and of him on tenter-hooks for a cup of tea, yet helpless because he could not make it himself nor had he found anyone to make it for him. If mothers enjoy watching the clumsy drooling of their babes while they eat, or of their faltering attempts at walking, then I enjoyed, similarly, his helplessness in matters practical, his vulnerability when it came to ideas, his speechless need of me—and all this set off by an aloofness, a vast and serious knowledge based on self-sacrificing years of study and hard work, his refusal to concede, to compromise : all this I admired, perhaps envied.

In a sudden, impulsive longing to be with him, be close to him, I leapt up, full of decisions to make haste in undressing, preparing myself, then joining him at last; so that we could go out into the garden, together, where the beds had been made for the night and were cooling in the moonlight. But when I went to rouse him from the couch, with a touch, I saw that he had closed his eyes not with mere tiredness, but in profound, invulnerable sleep, and was very far from any world of mine, however enticing. I hesitated, wishing to summon him to me, yet knowing he could never join me. It was of no use. After all I sighed— and, once more, was sad.

So I went to change in silence, and, on the dressing-table, found the posy with which I had set out for the evening. A pink carnation bound to a red rose, both lifeless now, buried with the deeds and dust of the evening, already belonging to yesterday, corpses of today . . . like all the rest of the delights of which I had thought of speaking to Gautama about, in trying to convince him of the perfection of my world, and now seeing them as tainted with fatality. Fatality—fate. Fato—fatality. I fingered the flowers sadly, and felt much like them myself—bruised and tired, not quite alive, not quite of today. Throwing them down on the floor where they lay soft and limp, I remembered how, as we had driven home down a dark street I had seen a dark young woman in a crimson sari, holding a white dog on a leash, walk into a shuttered house, followed by a dark young man in white. At the door, she paused, turned and smiled at him, and he smiled in reply, and went up the steps behind her. The white dog, unsmiling, followed them in, and we swept past and away even before the door had shut behind them.

When I lay in bed at last, I continued to think of them, uneasily, restlessly, connecting them with a dream I had once had as a child, with the convoluted history behind a ruby red as blood, with the brief life of a painted butterfly. Butterfly, moon—moon rising, falling, now waning, now waxing. The eternal flux, the eternal decay of a world of rubies and butterflies. My inability to capture it, to hold it transfixed as an insect in amber, haunted me now, as did the image of the dark woman and the white dog in the dark lane, and the swiftly travelling, ever mutable moon above me, and I turned upon my bed, and turned again, till my fresh white nightclothes were damp with perspiration, the white sheets crumpled and comfortless. Upon this bed of hot, itching sand, I summoned up again the vision of the tenebrific albino who had cast his shadow like a net across me as I had fled down the corridor of years, from the embrace of protection to embrace of love, yet catching me as surely as a gaint fisherman striding through the shallows of moonlit seas, throws his fine net with one brief, expert motion and knows, as it settles with a falling whisper upon the still water, that he will find in it a catch : I had not escaped. The years had caught up, and now the final, the decisive one held me in its perspiring clasp from which release seemed impossible. And now I recalled that oil-slick, sibilant tongue whispering poetry to me in the bat-tortured dark. 'Do you not hear the peacocks call in the wilds ? Are they not blood-chilling, their shrieks of pain ? "*Pia, pia,*" they cry. "Lover, lover. *Mio, mio,*—I die, I die." Go out into the jungles before the monsoons come—at the time when the first clouds cross the horizon, black as the kohl in your grave eyes. How they love the rain— these peacocks. They spread out their splendid tails and begin to dance, but, like Shiva's, their dance of joy is the dance of death, and they dance, knowing that they and their lovers are all to die, perhaps even before the monsoons came to an end. Is it not agony for them ? How they stamp their feet, and beat their beaks against the rocks ! They will even grasp the snakes that live on the sands there, and break their bodies to bits against the stones, to ease their own pain. Have you seen peacocks make love, child ? Before they mate, they fight. They will rip each other's breasts to strips and fall, bleeding, with their beaks open and panting. When they have exhausted them- selves in battle, they will mate. Peacocks are wise. The hundred eyes upon their tails have seen the truth of life and death, and know them to be one. Living, they

95

are aware of death. Dying, they are in love with life. "Lover, lover," you will hear them cry in the forests, when the rain-clouds come, "Lover, I die" . . .'

And the rain-clouds, emerged again from the horizon that was eternally pregnant with promise at one end, and at its opposite pole, was an eternally hungry and open grave. In the shadows I saw peacocks dancing, the thousand eyes upon their shimmering feathers gazing steadfastly, unwinkingly upon the final truth—Death. I heard their cry and echoed it. I felt their thirst as they gazed at the rain-clouds, their passion as they hunted for their mates. With them, I trembled and panted and paced the burning rocks. Agony, agony, the mortal agony of their cry for lover and for death.

As a child, I had gone for walks in wild tracts of land that might now be cultivated, calmed, divided into quiet bungalows with formal gardens, but to me they remain eruptions of rock and wilderness. There were great boulders there with stark gaps in which snakes and lizards lived lives as quick and brief as their heart-beats. There were tangles of thorn-bushes that, in certain seasons, bore small, poignant flowers, in other hard, sapless berries with large stones for hearts. I roamed the rocklands in search of them, and of brown hares and porcupine quills, and often I came across a single majestic peacock trailing over a bronze boulder its long, burdensome tail, glittering and gleaming in a thousand shades of carbon-blue and green and lamp-black. Sometimes I saw a flurry of small, tortured peahens, drab, colourless, though, in their brown breasts, their hearts were great and rich with scarlet blood. They lived lives so inverted, so

96

given to passions of which I knew nothing, that I merely wondered at their strange colours, their many-eyed feathers, and covered my ears when they shrieked. But, later, after the astrologer entered my life, on soundless feet, I would lie in bed in my sleeping home, and listen for those calls from rock and jungle lands, even after I had forgotten why I listened for them. When I heard one cry in the stillness of night, its hoarse, heart-torn voice pierced my white flesh and plunged its knife to the hilt in my palpitating heart. 'Lover, I die.' Now that I understood their call, I wept for them, and wept for myself, knowing their words to be mine.

Not only their words, but their fate. And now, once more, I strained to hear them calling on the Ridge, that rocky wasteland—a romantic hideout of storms, sunsets, wilderness—that crosses Old Delhi, and is peopled with rabbits and porcupines, and the snakes and peacocks of my childhood, as well as burning Flame of the Forest trees and secret robber caves and crumbling Moghul ruins. Had I heard one, I believe I should have expired, for my heart was so stretched with fear, that one small droplet of sound in it would have strained it to bursting. Listened to it pound, and twisted on my bed, crying the peacock's cry. And I knew I should never again sleep in peace. For, God, now I was caught in the net of the inescapable, and where lay the possibility of mercy, of release ? This net was no hallucination, no. In the day-time, amidst companions, I could force myself into believing that it was only a nightmare, no more. But, in the night, under the stark gaze of the moon, in that waiting silence, my memories came to life, were so vivid, so detailed, I knew them to be real, too real. Or is it madness? Am I gone insane? Father! Brother! Husband! Who is my saviour? I am in need of one. I am dying, and I am in love with living. I am in love, and I am dying. God, let me sleep, forget, rest. But no, I'll never sleep again. There is no rest any more—only death and waiting.

4

The soft blue twilight in the garden vibrated with rich words like *'zulph'* and *'mehtab'*—words filled with the short, deep sighs of *weltschmerz*, and rounded with a passion for balance, design, precision. They seemed to issue out of the mouths of the large, white flowers that had begun to breathe now in the evening dimness, out of the beds of earth, freshly dug and moistly odorous. The first star trembled into etiolated life and somewhere the promise of a moon turned upon the green air and stirred. There might have been no one in the round cup of the leaf-shrouded garden on that still, damp, bat-wing scimitared evening, no one but those who were part of it, of the leaves and the earth—the worms and crickets and small, sleeping birds. Yet I was only too aware of the relaxed, comfortable figures clothed in fine, white muslin, sunk into the depths of the old, wicker chairs. In the mirror over the mantelpiece in the drawing-room, I could decipher, in that blurred pool of crepuscular shade, the movements of elegant white sleeves, idle fingers reaching towards glasses that gleamed, beacon-like, on the tables beside them, tops of heads, blunt and blank as owls' faces in

98

daylight. I heard the hearty laughter that divorced them from the still, brooding Old Delhi garden, and then strings of liquid words, gem-like and fluent as notes of a flute falling one upon the other, which stitched them to the summer evening again.

Restlessly, I paced up and down in the hot, closed room where an electric light switched on would have set fire to the parched, aching wood and stifling fibre. I did not wish to meet those men who had not cared to have me come out to them—but I longed to be outdoors ; their alien laughter irked me, yet the basic passions and tragedies they spoke of, in quoted couplets, appealed to me with equal strength. I was caged in this room that I hated—severe, without even the grace of symmetry. I walked to and fro, fingering the few objects of value and loveliness that it contained— all of them presented to me by my father, chosen by his forefathers. 'Your knick-knacks,' Gautama, who saw no value in anything less than the ideas and theories born of human and, preferably, male brains, sometimes said, to cruelly tease. 'Designed to gather dandruff and defeat your feather-duster,' he would say, blowing dust through the crack of a small, bronze Shiva's elbow, and 'What purpose do they serve ?' opening a small lacquer box and finding it empty save for a bent pin. And I, remembering them in their glory; catching the pollinated sunshine upon gleaming teakwood bookshelves, freckled with the shredded shadows of bowls of tuberoses, now pitied them in their shame, and did my best to polish them and restore their rightful pride. But that glory had died under such treatment, and the wood felt very like wood to my fingers, the lacquer very like lacquer. Though, perhaps, the dancing Shiva was smiling still, faintly, inscrutably in the twilight, as he listened to familiar words, to familiar flights of Persian fancy. Familiar, for they had been quoted so often on the lawns at home, and in the echoing drawing-rooms. 'No language more evocative,' my father had said, turning the finely worked pages of a book of *ghazals* as he read to me. 'No language more aristocratic.' Following upon his musing came a fluting dew-descent of just such words as he had spoken of, flooding the dark with their black brilliance.

I can no longer swear to the words of this couplet which aroused such a flurry of applause from my husband's friends in the garden, but I know it was one that sounded familiar to my ears, and which I connected with my father, with a dazzling summer night, a gathering of friends on the terrace, with a sweet ache in my elbows as I propped myself up on the windowsill behind a dense rose trellis and strained to listen, to steal a little of the treasure which so enraptured these wise, cultured, elderly aristocrats who hovered over my childhood like kindly patrons. Drawn by this remembrance of an intoxicating night that was deepened into a ringing hollow by a profound and adoring love for the quoter of the lovely couplet—my father, I wandered to the door to peer into the purple twilight where wreaths of cigar smoke wound white circles around immaculate white clothing and effulgent white blossoms. Gautama was laughing. He who remained always untouched, unscalded, was entertained by the sight of his more sentimental cronies swaying their heads and uttering deep cries of pleasure upon hearing a verse that to him sounded absurdly primitive, naive and pointless, although he was no less keen an admirer than they of the symmetry of concentrated form, the exquisite choice of exquisite words. I heard them reprove him for his insouciant amusement, I heard him reply with light sarcasm. They accused him of philistinism, tried to convince him of the glory of pure verse, each by quoting what he felt to be the best and the most dazzling in Urdu poetry. He laughed.

'The stagnant dregs of a sentimentalism available only to the decadent.' He damned them with one blow, and even I winced.

'*Paimana*,' mused an ecstatic voice, lost on the swaying sea of a word which he repeated to himself so ecstatically. '*Tamanna*.'

'This plague of philistines,' growled another, bitterly, and Gautama laughed and rose to refill their glasses.

Spreading my arms out before me, I felt a stormy longing to rush out and join them, fling myself upon the dew-wet grass and beg them to continue, to roll out, breaker upon breaker, this ocean of rich, thick red wine, perhaps also, perhaps most of all, for my father's presence amongst them, his hand placed gracefully on the chair's arm, his voice, gentlest and deepest of all. But I also knew that nothing would have angered Gautama more, and Gautama angered when already in this astringent, ironic temper would be a catastrophe to me, who dreaded the rift of a quarrel now when we needed to ally ourselves so closely together, to withstand the threat that loomed over our unity. I withdrew heavily from the door, and flung myself at the mantelpiece, to cling to it and gaze into the mirror, knowing that my desire to hear this long-loved poetry quoted by cigar-musty, male voices was mingled with a deeper, stronger instinct to spend each possible moment close to Gautama, and cleave to him before we were cleaved by violence. In the watery reflection, I tried in vain to make out which one of the vague blurs he was, which arm was his, which sharp, incisive gesture. As it was, his voice came to me disembodied, from another world, and the fear that I felt more and more frequently and desperately now, overcame me with a rush. Already we belonged to separated worlds, and his seemed the earth that I loved so, scented with jasmine, coloured with liquor, resounding with poetry and warmed by amiability. It was mine that was hell. Torture, guilt, dread, imprisonment—these were the four walls of my private hell, one that no one could survive in long. Death was certain.

Then—from this secret so subtly revealed to me upon the dark breath of twilight—was I to deduce that these were the destinies that had been chosen for us ? That Gautama was the one fated to live on in this world that daily grew more desirable, and I the one to writhe and die in the cruellest of hells ?

Under the onrush of this ghastly revelation, came the undercurrent of another searing realization—that it was not only for his presence, his love that I longed, but mainly for the life that would permit me to touch him, feel his flesh and hair, hold and then tighten my hold on him. And not on Gautama alone, but on all the pulsating world around him, from the frieze of stars silently exploding in the summer sky to the faintly fluttering owls making covert, hidden love in the crotch of the fig tree—all that suggested life and the great, entrancing world to me who was doomed not to live.

It was the first time that I admitted to the limitations of love, and I flushed now that I realized it, yet I was in too agitated a state of mind to reflect long upon the shamefulness of this false love that I proclaimed. Racing through my veins was a drunken desire to rush out to my husband, to feel the scratching and tickling of live grass beneath my feet, to smell the sprinkled earth and tobacco, to listen to the words of those who, too, had been drunk with life as with wine. What if this were the last evening in which to enjoy the ecstasy of being alive ! What if tomorrow I were a mere stone, mute, immobile, extinct ? For now I knew my destiny. It was annihilation. Annihilation, I repeated, trembling.

Ringing with sympathy, a gentle voice drifted towards me like a fellow inmate in a nightmare asylum, coming to console.

'Lord, thou hast dealt me so many sorrows,
To bear them, couldst thou not also have lent me another heart ?'

It was an indication of a welcome, a beckoning and an opening of doors—unmistakable, surely ? Certain, foolishly certain of this, I found myself rushing out and appearing breathlessly in their midst—the midst of this charmed circle of leisurely gentlemen, so comfortably, securely male, laughing, talking, drinking, genially drinking themselves into delight. I was, thereupon, rebuffed, rebuked, rejected. Politely they rose to their feet, well-manneredly they greeted me, enquired after my health, vacated a place for me, tried, however painfully, to continue anxiously, their line of bliss where an hysterical woman had no out. It was place. Yet it was not they who turn

103

Gautama. Turning his back to me, he stood talking to a friend, a glass in his hand, and his voice rose, in order that I might hear, when he said, 'Blissful, yes, because it is unrelated to our day, unclouded by the vulgarity of ill-educated men, or of overbearing women. . .'

Did I deserve that ? Did I really deserve that ? I moaned, leaning a febrile forehead upon the cool mirror—the mirror, always the mirror !—in my bedroom, feeling sick, as though I had been struck a blow, knocked giddy. Was it so unforgivable to wish to share in human friendliness ? In companionship ? To Gautama it was—for a woman, for a light-headed woman, a childish one, like myself. In his world there were vast areas in which he would never permit me, and he could not understand that I could even wish to enter them, foreign as they were to me. On his part, understanding was scant, love was meagre. Not to be loved as one does love. . .

In the flashing darkness of eyeballs pressed upon by wet fingers, I relived the horror of those awesome realizations that had followed, sometimes, a moment of union, and taught me how hopeless, how impotant is sex—where not union but communion is concerned. 'Gautama,' I had whispered then, torn to shreds by the dragon-like dark, and my worn body had made a movement towards him. 'Yes ?' he had replied, in a voice daylit, so styptic, so dry, that we might never burshed hand with hand, twined hair with hair, ev the most private night. Or else, 'What now ?' B I could not bear to think of that. Or of momen en I had yearned for the contact that goes deep flesh—that of thought—and longed

104

to transmit to him the laughter that gurgled up in my throat as I saw a goat nuzzle, secretly, a basket of sliced melons in the bazaar while the vendor's back was turned, or the profound thrill that lit a bonfire in the pit of my stomach when I saw the sun unfurl like a rose in the west, the west and farther west. . .But those were the times when I admitted to the loneliness of the human soul, and I would keep silent. The things we leave unsaid would fill great volumes ; what we do say, only the first few pages of introduction. The silence descended upon me again now, and while I held my soul, still burning, in my hands, I saw my body detach itself from it and float away, to rest upon the dim mirror where I could gaze upon it from a cool distance. I studied it, absorbed : the round, childish face, pretty, plump and pampered, its smooth, silken skin with one, small velvet mole ; the small, shell-like ears curling around petty ignorance ; the soft, overful lips arched with vulnerable sweetness ; the long, curled lashes and the very heavy, very dark black brows ; the silly collection of curls, a flower pinned to them—a pink flower, a child's choice of a posy. One might think it a lovable face. But it was not the face that a man like Gautama could love. He might be charmed by it, momentarily, diverted by it, for a while, but to capture him entirety, if a fleshly face could do it, it would have to be a finer one, the elongated, etiolated one of an intellectual, refined by thought and reflection, bereft of the weakness of impulses, aloof from coarseness and freshness. This I told myself in calm, still words, and I gazed long at each feature of the image before me, so like painting on a chocolate box, and hated in fier. Hate was a new emotion to me, and, in trespassing upon it, I entered a new vista of knowledge. I forced myself into believing that I could see now what must be the reason for my hating it so, for Gautama's spurning it —visible to our subconscious only. It must be a mark upon my forehead, which had been so clear to the opaque eye of the albino who had detected it, upon which the stars now hurled themselves vengefully, and which prophesied a relentless and fatal competition between myself and Gautama. I tried to define this mark, give it a name, a locality. Was it an arrow ? A coffin ? A cross ? A star ? Was it between the eyes ? At the temple ? Was it dark ? Was it pale ? And what made gods reach out and touch it with their cold fingers, as they considered the prospect of a murder ?

Murder.

Shocked as though I had truly found a blemish in my unscarred skin, I drew away from the mirror with a shudder. I could no longer bear to see that clear, ignorant and insane face, and looked away, down at the rows of little gleaming crystal bottles of perfume and *attar*, *sindoor* and *kum-kum*. In a damp, white handkerchief, gathered into a nest, lay a heap of white jasmine buds that the gardener had plucked from the dawnfresh hedges that morning, for me to thread into garlands for my hair and wrists, and which, for some reason, I had forgotton. There they lay, almost palpitating with living breath, open, white, virginal. I plunged my face into them and kissed them with a wild longing to pierce through that unimpeachable, immaculate chastity of whiteness, to the very soul of their maddening fragrance. What dreams they conjured in sweet of scent, what passions, what scenes of love

106

and farewell. . .I tore myself away from them, having bruised them with my kisses, and trembling, flung them against the mirror, at that fleeting image to which they belonged, and backed out of the room which was now terrorized by the vast, purple shadows of a dreadful night.

Out on the verandah, the night air, however hot and oppressive, was clean, and I sank onto the steps that led down to the undisturbed back garden. I sat there a long while, forcibly dragging my mind away from that pivot of horror, by focussing, fastening its shreds carefully onto one peg of substantiality after another: the single white streak of cloud unfolding across the sky in one long line, the single white tube-rose that drooped with the weight of its own heavy, nocturnal scent, the thickness of the turgid air, still and uncreased by breezes, the vague distinctions between the black shapes of the oleander shrubs and the black masses of sky and shadow. A cricket chirped loudly quite close to me, and only when it fell silent did I glance down and see it sitting near my bare foot. The night fell still, the little cricket beside me fell still, and my heart fell still inside me.

At last it fell still. During all my rages of rebellion and terror, I waited for these pauses to follow, these intervals of calm. It was as though the thick, red blood that surged so violently inside my skull now ebbed away, seeping little by little away from the convolutions of my heated brain, leaving it, at last, washed, bathed, cleansed and calm. This is what the *sunnaysis* feel, I told myself, this is what a *yogi* makes himself feel. Fortunate, wise ones, they know how much safer, how much more restful it is than the turmoil of a life such as I held onto, so insanely. Insanely. I dropped my head into my hands. Yes, I am going insane. I am moving further and further from all wisdom, all calm, and I shall soon be mad, if I am not that already. Perhaps it is my madness that leads me to imagine that horoscope, that encounter with the albino, his predictions, my fate? Perhaps it is only a phenomenon of insanity? And insanity can be cured. . .

But, dully, in that quiet time, I had to admit that, at that moment, I was, and knew myself to be, quite, quite sane, in full possession of my senses and capable of recalling, with perfect clarity, the details of that ancient interview, my father's dread and fury, everything. It was no delirium. My suddenly sobered mind affirmed it a certainty, as the telescope affirms the certainty of the physical substance of those mysterious lights in the night sky, the planets. No fairy tales those, but proven.

And so I continued to insist, to assure, yet not daring to look up at a star for comfort—for no star could give me that, they had betrayed me, those vague, ethereal dimnesses of the night. And all the while I thought of Gautama too, of the party continuing on the front lawn. Had there been a bond between us, he would have felt its pull, I thought of him so deeply. But, of course, there was none. That had been proved to me tonight. There was no bond, no love—hardly any love. And I could not bear to think of that. Phrases came to me from the *Gita*, so long unread, that calmed me with their cool, steadfast wisdom.

'He is fit to attain immortality who is serene and not affected by these sensations, but is the same in pleasure and pain. . .'

108

'He whose mind is not agitated in calamities and who has no longing for pleasure, free from attachment, fear and anger, he indeed is said to be of steady wisdom. . .'

'He who is free from all attachment and neither rejoices on receiving good nor is vexed on receiving evil, his wisdom is well established. . .'

'When he completely withdraws his senses from sense objects as the tortoise withdraws its limbs, then wisdom becomes well established. . .'

And through these solid, simple, deeply consoling words that had remained, somehow, surprisingly fresh and crystalline in my untidy mind, there came the equally gentle, equally ancient strains of a *raga* played on a learner's sitar, from the neighbouring house where lived a family of genteel Bengalis whose daughters, each evening, took lessons in music. One studied the sitar, and ran her fingers up and down the sweet, tenuous wires as silver fishes flash in streams, while her sister's agile birdvoice ran up and down the scales, over and over again. 'Sa, re, ga, ma, pa, da, ni, sa. . .' it soared up fluently, then hung suspended, precariously, like a small gem tossed up into the air where it revolves, for a brief, hesitant second, before it comes plummeting down into the palm of one's hand. 'Sa,' it rang again, quivering at that awesome apex, and then, after this tiny conquest, came the tumbling descent, 'Sa, re, ga, ma, pa, da, ni, *sa—*' it sank to the very bottom of the night. Then followed a pause in which the very crickets held their breaths, but the plantains stirred, sighing, as though they were kept awake by the music lesson, and, in tune with their expectation, it began all over again.

It was trying, too piercing to be escapable, and I was forced to listen, to rise and fall with the obdurate movement of the music into the air, down to earth, into the air, and down again. Up and down the sitarist's fingers raced, and gaily the careless voice followed. I felt my heart rise to my mouth and fall to the pit of my stomach again, sickeningly, each time that clear voice descended, and I wondered how long I could bear this exhausting music that was not music to me, but the leitmotiv of my life, my destiny, strumming in my ears and racing in my blood.

But they were tireless, and I was swept along, up and down, with these sound patterns, and their associations that whirled around in the same spell-binding motion, so that Gautama's step entering it, did not break the line at all, but seemed a part of it, adding itself quite naturally. With him he brought an overwhelming odour of smoked cigars, of whisky, of manhood—to me, all inexpressibly attractive, so that I was nearly crying with weakness when he fondled my head, saying, 'Here you are, all by yourself. Why did you run away from us like that, silly girl?' He sat down on the step beside me, an unprecedented act of indulgence. With near fright, I withdrew from him, and gently he let go of my face : it was as though he had laid hold of my very heart, [the raw, blood-filled, living organ itself, and in drawing away. I might have taken the skin, the covering tissue with me, but I left the body of it in his hands, and felt his fingers around it still.

'You did not want me,' I whispered, choking, and clasped my hands as I felt that touch on my body yet, passing a pain into it.

'Not want you ? Did I say so? Did anyone say so? Why all this melodrama? I merely wondered what you could possibly want of a gathering of elderly men, all slightly inebriated, and speaking in Urdu. Besides, you embarrassed them rather.'

'I don't care! These old fogies need a bit of embarrassing—a bit of shaking up. All I wanted was to be outside—with you.' I turned to look at him then. 'Near you,' I added, and put out my hand to touch his cool white sleeve. 'But you made me go away,' I breathed, and drew back my hand without touching it.

He sighed, fumbled, lit himself a cigarette as though he had not heard me at all, were no longer aware of me. The small flame of the match lit the cave of his cupped hand into a ruby grotto, then was flung away into the dark where a startled frog croaked at it, and then it went out, the frog was silent, and there was only the insignificant glow of the cigarette left. Then Gautama shifted.

' "He who is free from all attachment",' he said. softly, ' " and neither rejoices on receiving good, nor is vexed on receiving evil, his wisdom is well established".'

'But,' I cried, 'That is from the *Gita*!'

'Of course', he said, turning to me, smiling. 'And you are surprised. Yet there was a time when it used to lie on your bed-table, and you would study it ferociously, every night.'

'The *Gita*,' I repeated, stammering. Had he turned mind-reader? How much did he know, unknown to me ?

'You have even forgotton those nights,' he said. 'And I was going to be your friend, philosopher and

111

guide tonight, and ask you to remember what it says of attachment, of the sins arising from it, and the payment for those sins. Listen. "Thinking of sense objects, man becames attached thereto. From attachment arises longing and from longing anger is born. From anger arises delusion ; from delusion, loss of memory is caused. From loss of memory the discriminative faculty is ruined and from the ruin of discrimination, he perishes".'

Somehow I listened to the end of it, bore it all down to the last word. And those echoed. 'He perishes'. Perishes. I felt my heart empty itself out. 'Yes,' I said, and even to me my voice sounded strange, sharp and stinging with bitterness. 'How it suits you to quote those lines of a dry stick—an inhuman dry stick. Oh, you know nothing, understand nothing.' I raised my voice. 'Nor will you ever understand. You know nothing of me—and of how I can love. How I *want* to love. How it is *important* to me. But you,' and I looked at him straight, and with hate, 'You've never loved. And you don't love me. . .'

'Now look—'

'Oh, if you do, if you say you do, it means nothing. Love has no importance for you. It is merely—attachment,' and I spat out that treacherous, betraying word, hating it.

'Love,' he said, surprised, unpleasantly surprised for he discarded his cigarette into the Queen of the Night bush, and clicked open his cigarette case as upon an unexpected new facet in a so far straightforword case, an unexpected and undesirable facet. 'Whoever spoke of love?' he said, drawing his fine eyebrows together so that his face drew into a mass of

112

complex lines. He looked very much the meditator beneath the *bo* tree, seated upon a soft tiger skin, too fastidious to touch the common earth, with those long, clean-cut hands of his, too fastidious to admit such matters as love, with its accompanying horror of copulation, of physical demands and even, overbearingly, spiritual demands of possession and rights won and established. . .

But no, tonight I would not admire him for this superior plane he always managed to elevate himself onto when I tried to involve him in my matters, my wants and cares, which to him were childish, tiresome and even distasteful. Tonight I would hold him down beside me. 'I speak of it,' I said loudly and the small white stars of the Queen of the Night bush released such overpowering fumes of fragrance, paradisiacal and unearthly, that I felt a little giddy, feverish even. 'And you will think me a tiresome child for it, for showing what you once called my "third-rate poetess's mind". . .'

'I never—'

'You did, and you believe it now. Because I love you. Because when you are away from me, I want you. Because I insist on being with you, being allowed to touch you and know you. You can't bear it, can you? No, you are afraid. You might—perish.' I laughed bitterly, bitterly.

'Listen,' he said, when he heard that laugh, and stood up abruptly so that he stood tall and stooped above me, his head in the stars, and I looked down at his feet.

'No,' I said, fiercely. '*You* listen to me tonight. You never will let me tell you this. Why? Are you

113

afraid? Because you cannot meet it? You feel out of your element? You can't bear to be—not alone?' I raced on till I was tired, and drooped. Then I touched the tip of his foot. 'Is there nothing,' I whispered, 'is there nothing in you that would be touched ever so slightly, if I told you I live my life for you?'

Immediately he bent, thrust my hands away, pulled me up and made me stand there, on the steps, two steps above him, so that our faces were at a level. We stared at each other, I looked at his face, the nostrils pinched with anger, the mouth tight with impatience. The moonlight dramatized it all, revealed lines and shadows, accentuated them. Nothing was hidden. All was revealed, and it was not what I hunted for. He was not on my side at all, but across a river, across a mountain, and would always remain so.

'There is nothing,' I breathed, half in question, half in statement. 'You are—untouched. How can I explain it to you then? I shall never be able to tell you now. You shall never help me. It is all true. One of us will win, the other must lose.'

'Listen,' he insisted, for my words made no sense to him, he was not a mind-reader at all, he had not the faintest knowledge of me. 'Listen. You do not need to explain. I understand, I do. And if I appear —untouched, then it is because I am too perturbed to be touched. This is madness, Maya, quite uncalled for . . .'

'Then I am mad ? You think me mad ?' I scream- ed, throwing up my fists to thrust him from me, flinging myself away from him, down the steps, into the dark, the dark. I began to cry. I did not care. I was outraged. Traitor ! I wanted to scream. Traitor,

114

you are the one to betray me !

He followed me, grasped me and shook me roughly. 'Neurotic', he said, 'Neurotic, that's what you are. A spoilt baby, so spoilt she can't bear one adverse word. Everyone must bring a present for little Maya—that is what her father taught her.' It was he who spoke bitterly now.

'Don't you speak of my father—'

'I will certainly speak of him. He is the one responsible for this—for making you believe that all that is important in the world is to possess, possess—riches, comforts, posies, dollies, loyal retainers—all the luxuries of the fairy tales you were brought up on. Life is a fairy tale to you still. What have you learnt of the realities ? The realities of common human existence, not love and romance, but living and dying and working, all that constitutes life for the ordinary man. You won't find it in your picture-books. And that was all you were ever shown—picture-books. What wickedness to raise a child like that !'

'I had the happiest childhood. They were my happiest times.'

'Yes, and all you ever knew was happiness. What a crime ! A crime because it was a delusion. And here you are, capable of seeing nothing but delusions, imagining them to be real. How prettily you stroll in your garden, dreaming of the fairies that sleep in the buds. . .'

'What do you—'

'And thinking of me as the wicked bogey-man who refuses to play along with you, who cuts down all the pretty posies with a lash of his whip. Don't cry. Don't, please, start crying, Maya. Listen, for once,

115

seriously, because I am speaking seriously. You must decide, you must see for yourself and realize what are the important things in life, what are the true values. That is why I am quoting the *Gita* so profusely to-night. I know you know it, and wish you would recall those lines, understand their meaning now, at last. Otherwise life will remain an emptiness to you and you will continue to reach out and grasp for every-thing—every desirable thing in view, and imagine you have filled your life and given meaning to your existence by doing so.' He took my arm, he urged me forward, and in a little while we were pacing the lawn, sedately, as though we were speaking of vegetables and the weather. His voice pattered on, the fall of cool leaves upon my burning self, burying me with their autumnal maturity, their experience and sobriety. 'I have always felt,' he said, 'the necessity in each human being for a—vocation. I must call it vocation for lack of a more *embracing* word. Strange,' he mused, and began upon another cigarette, 'strange how this evening began with Urdu poetry, and winds up in Hindu philosophy. Yes, it is definitely the night of the *Gita*. It has provided me with yet another quotation for you. "He who, controlling the senses of the mind, follows without attachment the path of action with his organs of action, he is esteemed." We are constantly being told of the risk in coveting the fruits of our actions, the merit of performing our actions without contemplating their success or failure. Action—or work, or life, whichever you please—of that order is what I mean by vocation. I am certain, experience makes me certain, that only those who are capable of this manner of living, and working, are

116

capable of peace, or serenity—better words than happiness, both of them.'

'Like you,' I said, with the last ember of bitterness flickering up in my mind which was growing steadily more dull and ashen with weariness. 'Like you and all your marvellous, hard-working family, I suppose.'

He chose to overlook the bitterness—that is, if he noticed it at all. 'Not at all, like my family or myself, Maya. We are egoists, one and all. We work for fame, name, money, all the other evils put together. Yet we do have our work—our vocations—each one of us, and so far, I must say, it appears to have brought us a certain amount of serenity. Not the complete ideal peace the *Gita* tells us about, not by any means, but perhaps a larger amount of it than most people have.'

'But I am not like you, I am different from all of you.'

'That is true,' he granted me, without looking at me, gazing, instead, into the shadows. 'If one is not of the detached temperament, it is rather more difficult to live detachedly. Yes, I grant you that. Yet, if one must have a real, solid, personal world, why not create one within oneself, to detach oneself into when the world around one grows either too boring or too hectic ?"

'But I am not like that,' I insisted, beginning to whine now, yet feeling my innate sequaciousness rise like a flood tide within me and begin to drown, little by little, my struggling protests. It was immensely wearing, but also drowsily comforting. 'I don't care to detach myself into any other world than this. It isn't boring for me. Never boring. I suppose I get

117

much more out of it than you do. Could *you* sit here, on the steps, without a book, without a piece of paper even, just looking at the trees and thinking about them ?'

'Lord, no !' he said, in horror.

'But, you see, I can. I have so much to look at, to touch, and feel, and—be happy about. I like to walk about here and touch things—leaves, sticks, earth, everything. I play with my cat. And if I am lonely, I can visit my friends. The world is full—*full*, Gautama. Do you know what that means ? I am not bored with it that I should need to hunt another one !'

He glanced at me with a sideways glance. His interest was aroused as it could occasionally be, not by the opinion expressed or the theory expounded by a person, but by the person himself. It was still an analytic, cool, searching interest, but interest it was, and, perhaps because there was, after all, greater intimacy in our relationship than in any other he was involved in, there was a certain solicitude in his interest, which was tender, and an appraisal, which was new.

'You are quite right,' he said, stamping his cigarette underfoot, so that we were completely in the dark and aware of the moon that had risen above the roof, like a shallow vessel, a golden boat in the sky, brilliantly polished and richly vivid. 'You are right. You are, in a fashion, less of an egoist than I. While I must always have a piece of paper in my hand, or a book, or people around me, so that I may write of myself, search for myself in them, talk to them of myself, you are the one who can bear to be absolutely
118

alone, losing yourself in your garden and your pets. Strange,' he mused, turning away from me and beginning upon a nervous chain of cigarettes, half or quarter smoked, that seemed to be necessary fuel for his ticking brain. 'Strange, because then you should be capable of far greater detachment than I, hence of greater peace of mind and stability. That is the end of our philosophical aspirations—to exist like a lily upon water, rooted in water yet with its petals dry, untouched by it. The lamp placed in a windless corner, unflickering. The tortoise with its limbs withdrawn from the external world—oh, the entire cult of symbols that we have for this ideal existence. But who is capable of it ? I, with my books, my work, or you with your sensual pleasure in living ? Christ, who went out into the world to mingle with people, acquaint himself with their suffering, and involved himself in a series of miracles whereby to bring about physical well-being and salvation, or Buddha who meditated beneath the *bo* tree, his eyes closed to death, misery, pleasure, the temptation of helping, the temptation of saving, the temptation of attaining success ? A question that has employed thinking minds for centuries. The answer of course is there—in the *Gita*—once again, the *Gita*. "He whose joy is within, and whose light is within, that Yogi, being well-established in Brahman, attains to absolute freedom." The freedom of the lotus from water, of the lamp from winds, of the tortoise from all contact. Detachment—in a word, detachment.'

'And love ?' I broke in. 'And love ?'

'Love ? Love that is without any ambition, without any desire, without any life except that which

119

keeps it alive, burning, yes, that is well. But do you not, Maya,' and he touched my shoulder now, tenderly, 'mistake attachment for love ? And there lies your egoism after all. To meditate upon the garden on a fine evening—well, that is fine indeed. To throw oneself into a passion over a flower that is going to be dead by night, that is folly. From a passion of wonder and excitement you are led surely to a passion of unhappiness in its loss, depression and disillusionment. Therefore, to train yourself to remain detached— untouched, as you yourself called it—is worth a try, isn't it ? To train oneself, yes, to discipline oneself· Our yogis do it, and our *sunnyasis*, the true ones. And so they are free from disillusionment, and being free from that, are also free from any danger of perishing. That, I expect, is the eternity each religion yearns for, visualizing it with varying degrees of perspicacity. . .'

We wandered on, sometimes touching, then drawing apart, and, for once, I listened to him, listened fully and attentively. The dryness, the bleakness of his voice, of his theories, no longer bored me, or repelled me. I saw them now as a mass of rock, a large and steadfast rock, high and dry in middle of a tossing sea. To hold to it was safety. To be borne away from it, by my insane passions, my weaknesses and lack of control, was—to perish.

'Yet,' I murmured, sadly, 'to have known it—to have known that fine evening, that flower, isn't that something, Gautama? Isn't it?'

'Here,' he said, suddenly stopping. 'Here's one for you,' and he plucked a flower out of a bush, from somewhere, at random, and handed it to me. 'Who should deny you that?' he said, and smiled at me as to a winsome child.

I cupped my hands over it, with such care that my fingers nearly cracked beneath the stress. 'Do you know,' I said, 'I shouldn't mind dying now, after all. At this very moment. Then it would remain like this, for me. We should never walk a step farther, or say a single other word. It would all come to a stop here, and rest. Gautama, don't you wish it?'

He touched my arm and made me continue with our steady pacing. 'Yes,' he said, but in a tone once more distant and styptic. 'The tragedy of love is not what so many imagine it to be—the impossibility of maintaining it at its first exalted level. It is, as you have just indicated, the impossibility of remaining there briefly enough—so briefly that death cuts short, with one quick blow, this fated love, before the cancer has a chance to set in. But then, would one be strong enough to bear a life consisting of one splendid nova after the other, exploding magnificently and dazzlingly all the time? I think not. One is too weak. One wearies, one feels inadequate to its divinity, and so one chooses, rather, to drift along the downword stream. It is less tiring than fighting the sea, a wild sea. We aren't made to fight the tide, the current, one cannot remain always on the crest of the wave, the edge of the waterfall. One needs to breathe.'

'But,' I said, curving my fingers across the cold petals of the flower in my hand, with care, so as not to bruise it, 'how can one bear it changing? how can one bear to think of it all changing and dying, and never being the same again? It is always a loss.'

'What an Occidental you are,' he said, laughing.

121

'Your conception of life as one brief episode into which all experience, all success, all virtue must be crammed, for it is, alas, so short,' he cried, affecting a wail of self-pity to make me laugh. 'Where did you pick it up? Surely, coming from a family of God-fearing Brahmins, you have heard of a different conception, of life not as a spark that is once lit and then extinguished in purgatorial ashes, or, if one is virtuous and has behaved oneself, lives on amongst a blaze of other little sparks in a heaven that must be, by now, so ferociously illuminated as to necessitate the wearing of dark glasses, but of life as a constant glow, an aura that passes thorugh a continual cycle, passing from day to night, from the Manifest to the Unmanifest, and from the Unmanifest into the Manifest again. This life you speak of, this little episode, this brief flash-in-the-pan, how insignificant and trivial it appears compared with this immortal cycle to which all humanity is bound, living or dying, and which turns without stop, without *point*, you might say. . .'

'Yes,' I murmured, 'yes,' caressing the flower, feeling the grass prickle, feeling security lap me, safety and peace. A lovely vision was being created for me, and I half-closed my eyes and dreamt.

His voice penetrated. 'You will say—what, are we bound to this cycle then, tethered to it? But that is fatalism.' Now my attention was ance more fully with him, alert like a cobra spreading its hood at the first faint sound of approching danger. 'Ah, but see the logic of it—the perfect logic of it: one incarnation acting upon the other, the action performed in one incarnation bearing fruit in the next, as surely as autumn must follow summer, as surely as the rising tide must ebb. Knowing this, knowing that our deeds have significance, meaning, our lives develop an impetus without which life would be one amorphous darkness. . .'

'No!' I cried out, flinging out my hand to grasp that rock, and finding it gone, vanished beneath a heaving mass of waves that now rolled over my head with the thunder of drums. 'No!' Where were safety, reassurance gone? Peace? Gautama? He was betraying me: having led me to calm water, he now left me to drown in a treacherous sea. The dark, the sound of drums—all closed in on me, suffocating me, and I began to perspire. 'No!'

'Why?' he said, irritated at the interruption rather than suspicious of calamity. 'Why, where do you see the flaw? Which other religion will provide you with logic? Not faith, but logic ? Point out, if you are able. . .'

'Not faith but logic,' I repeated, stammering. 'But, Gautama, that is terrible—not faith, but logic.'

'Good God!' he cried, throwing up his hands. 'Are you, after all, one of those females who will, each day, bathe and clothe their plaster gods and goddesses, and feed them with sweetmeats, making yourself believe in their life, when your logic tells you they are made of mud and it is your hungry children who are real? Dear God, Maya, to discover this in someone who has lived with you for years—'

'But, Gautama, I cried, 'what have you said?' I turned to stare at him, see his face in white moonlight, but we were in the shadow of the limes. The limes of the dead Toto. 'To think—to think that we are to pay, in this life, for what we *may* have done in a past

123

one, to think that we may have to pay horribly, oh, horribly, for something terrible, something terrible, that we *might* have done—it is terrible!

'Stop saying terrible, terrible, horrible, horrible,' he said, exasperated. 'Here I give you the one acceptable explanation of suffering, of what we call, at times, "injustice", meaning, thereby, poverty, pain, deprivation, and you—'

'All punishment!'

'What an Occidental view of the theory of reincarnation. However, punishment might not be an entirely incorrect word to use, since that is often the form Karma takes in our eyes. But our vision is so hopelessly limited. If we could only widen it with finer logic, with greater faith in logic, with better memories —memory, the keynote to logic! How much a truly excellent memory could solve, could it pursue us from one existence to another. It seems to me it would make Karma not only more explicit but also. . .'

'Gautama', I whispered, gripping his arm, gripping it tight, and finding it flesh and bone, ashes and dust, not rock, not eternal rock at all. 'But Gautama, please—'

'Now what is it?' he sighed, in utter disgust. 'Really, it is quite impossible to talk to a women.'

'I'm going in', I said, in a small voice, for now I could hear a louder one, the one of rolling drums.

'By all means do,' he said, shaking himself free from my grasp, and then, suddenly, catching hold of my wrist. 'Why is your head so hot?' he asked suspiciously. 'And damp. Do you have a temperature?'

'No,' I said, 'No, Gautama, no temperature,' and began to move away from him, towards the house.

'Are you sure?' he called after me.
'Sure', I whispered, 'sure.'

5

'But to perish? Who? Tell me who.'

Gautama woke up. 'What is it?' he said, and held me in his arms. 'What is it, Maya? What are you dreaming of?'

After I had let myself be soothed by his fleshly presence, I turned away from him. He was hot, unbearably hot. So was my bed. The sprinkled earth had dried even in the moonlight. My tongue was thick with thirst. It seemed to me that death was, after all, very real, very probable. 'Terrible,' I sighed, pushing and pushing my hair from my face. 'Not to know. It is terrible, Gautama.'

'Your skin is burning—it's covered with prickly heat. Poor girl, it's a bad night. Shall we go indoors and try and sleep under the fan?'

'No,' I screamed. 'Not indoors. That fan—terrible!'

'You are still dreaming,' he said. 'Lie down and I'll fetch you a glass of water.'

'It will be hot.'

'No, cold water,' he said, and went to the earthen jar that stood on the verandah where the breeze could cool it, and tipped it over, I heard the water gurgle out, fresh and willing, into a tumbler. It smelt of wet earth and was as cool as moss. When I had drunk it, Gautama dipped his handkerchief in what remained at the bottom of the tumbler and wiped my face. The dampness prickled across my skin like so many bubbles rising to the surface and bursting. A parasite life, creeping across me. Frantically, I wiped it dry on my pillow.

'Don't do that, it'll make you hot all over again,' he said, 'try and sleep now. You're tired, I can see.'

'No,' I said. 'If I sleep, it'll come on me from behind. Gautama, watch over me,' I begged, gripping his hand. 'Help me keep awake.'

'Yes,' he said. 'Yes, Maya.'

'It is dangerous to sleep,' I said, and, clutching his hand, fell asleep as though I had been gassed.

Rats will suckle their young most tenderly. I know this, as now I lived quite near one, with seven young ones nestling between her legs. It may seem strange, incredible, yet no stranger than that the god whirling upon the torchlit stage, steps down, flings away the mask of viridian green and dead white, flings it away quite gracelessly, and reveals himself as an aged monkey, going flabby now, and perspiring, so that a foul stench surrounds him. And the god who leaps and whirls by torchlight, rules over the four-cornered *diva* with its flickering copper flames, and the aged monkey, hairy about the ears, are one. He even clears his throat and spits. But then, long ago I knew of snakes that coil themselves around the sweet-smelling sandalwood trees of the forest. Queen of the Night attracts snakes too, and tuberoses. All white flowers, chaste sweet white flowers, luring the snakes to their hearts of scent. And they come, the snakes, they come slithering towards these virgins of the night, with only their small cold eyes glinting in the dark, and they cling to the bending stalk, and with forked tongues lash and lash again at the heart of innocence.

One never knows but one may bend to look into the yellow pollen upon a fragile stamen and be struck between the eyes, deeply and fatally, by a viper's fang. One never knows but one may applaud a dancer and then find him a perspiring, asthmatic, flapjawed ape. And the rats with their young, suckling them, then lashing their tails, spreading plague. One must be careful for one never knows. Careful then, oh doubly, triply careful.

The desert too. Nothing but sand, they tell you, arid sand for mile upon fulvous mile. Loneliness, peace, speckless skies, pure and clear. So they say. But what of the dangers? Ah, they'll not tell you of them. Of the lizards, the lizards that come upon you, stalking you silently, upon clawed toes, slipping their clublike tongues in and out, in and out with an audible hiss and a death's rattle, slowly moving up, closing in on you, taking their time, knowing they have hypnotized you with their circular eyes, the centres of black glittering within circles of white, that they have struck you to a pillar of salt which, when it is motionless they will mount and lash with their slime-dripping tongues, lash and lash again, as they grip you with curled claws, rubbing their cold bellies upon yours, rubbing and grinding, rubbing and grinding. . .

Albinoes. Bleached into albinoes by the desert sun, these lizards. But the rat, too, is an albino, from having lived always in the dark, from never having seen the sun at all.

And moonlight ?

Ah, dangerous, if you don't know. Be careful, best be careful. Who knows which one is to perish? Perish one must. The desert is waiting, the rats and the lizards. They'll claim the flesh, the winds will carry the bones away. Mind the wind. Shut the windows. Hide, hide. Ah, here it comes, the lizard. Here it comes to mount you, saliva falling in lines of white from its mouth, its belly dragging on the ground, then dragging on you. Here it is.

'What are those lizards called, Gautama—the big ones that walk on their toes? Like alligators, almost.'

'Iguanas?' '

'Iguanas!' My blood ran cold, and I heard the slither of its dragging tail even now, in white daylight. 'Get off—I tell you, get off ! Go !'

'What is the matter?' said Gautama, putting down his tea-cup. 'I thought you liked her,' and he glanced at the cat who retired, offended, to a corner, her amber-green eyes half-slit, to lick her paws and clean her ears.

'Oh, I do,' I cried, overcome with remorse, and ran to her. 'Oh my lovely one, I do,' I insisted, rubbing my cheek on the top of her head and holding her soft, sequacious body against my neck. 'But she is so hot,' I complained. 'Go,' and I pushed her away again.

'You look hot. Why don't you drink lemon-juice instead of tea ?'

'No. No, no. Where is the postman ? Why won't he come ? He *knows* I am waiting so.' I went to the window and raised the bamboo screen. The morning light struck me like a white-hot block of heavy metal. 'Hot, already hot,' I cried, and let the screen drop. A pair of sparrows flew off with a whirr of disturbed wings, and a cloud of dust arose, yellow and grained. '*Why* can't that man dust properly,' I said, exasperated.

'Do it yourself one day, show him how,' said

128

Gautama drily.

'Myself?' I spun around to glare at him with hostility. 'In this heat? You want me to do the servants' work, in this heat?'

'If you think of nothing but the heat, it will make it worse for you.'

'Oh, it is the worst month. If only there would be a storm. It would be cool, at least for one night. If only the postman would come.'

'Why? Who is going to write to you?'

'Nobody!' I shouted, flinging myself down on the chair under the futile fan. 'Nobody writes to me. Not even father—and I'm waiting to hear from him about his plans for the summer. He *knows* I'm waiting.'

The servant came in with more tea, and there was no more talk, the only sounds were that of the aged fan gasping as it swung tiredly around, and of Gautama eating—of Gautama slicing papaya with a long knife, of him chopping a lemon in halves, squeezing it, of him sprinkling sugar, scattering some on the table, of him digging the spoon into the soft livid flesh, over-ripe, digging into it, digging it out, eating, eating.

'How can you eat in this heat? It sounds like a million caterpillars at it together.'

'I give up!' he moaned, and left for the office. The servant came in again to clear the table, shut all the windows, draw all the curtains. The house was still, darkened. I sat as in a tomb.

I sat, as in a tomb, on my small bamboo chair, resting my cheek upon my hand, waiting. There was nothing to look at. The fine shafts of light that stole through the bamboo screens remained still, unflicker-

129

ing. The warm breeze of the fan raised the edge of a folded newspaper, laid it down again. There was nothing for me to do. The heat grew and expanded in that closed room as a great, painful swelling in a womb, an immobile foetus, breathless with expectation and horror of all that was to come. There was all that to contemplate—yes : the horror of all that was to come. No, no, I would not think of that. Deliberately I twisted away from it, and thought how, in my father's house, there was a large ice-box under the white-painted stairs, and all day long one could fetch oneself long, cold drinks of lemon and mango, tamarind and passion-fruit. On blocks of ice the fruit lay gathering beads of frost, their ripe, burning cheeks cooling till they were fit to be eaten. Peaches, sent in baskets of straw from the hills, and apricots. Mangoes by the score, and lichees in bunches of prickly red, their leaves stiff and grey on long stalks. Loquats from the garden where they glowed golden against the glossy leaves in the evening, when it was cooler, and twilight fell, and one could venture out in fresh cottons, with flowers in one's hair—jasmine, *chameli, champa, bela,* all white and fragrant, plucked as buds onto a large brass tray at dawn, and kept fresh under wet muslin all day, till I would thread them into long chains, sitting on the swing-chair on the verandah with my needle and thread, and then wind them into my hair for the evening. The sound of water being sprayed across the lawn, of taps gurgling generously, of crickets stirring into life, drinks, sherbets, fruits on trees, on ice. Stars, on nights when the beds were brought out on the terrace upstairs, rose vines banking the parapet, and, from the lawn below, the drifting voices of my father and his friends reciting Persian couplets to each other, or one of them singing his soul away in a voice hoarse with passion and alcohol, till the night drew close to a palpitant dawn. Stars at dawn. Summertime at home.

At eleven o'clock, quite punctually, the servant brought me a glass of whipped buttermilk, spiced with cardamom, as I liked it, and a letter on a try. But not from father. A strange letter, of thick paper, and long, and with a foreign stamp. I studied it long before I realized it was an American stamp, and I screwed up my eyes before I could decipher the post-mark in that subdued semi-darkness. New York. New York?

Oh, Arjuna, to have written at last, after all this time.

'Arjuna !' I cried. 'Arjuna !' and banged on the window, then strained to see where he went. But he disappeared down an unlit alley on his rusty bicycle, the car swept me on, home from a tea-party. I did not tell father I had seen him in the bazaar. One never knew where Arjuna went, exactly. His departures and arrivals were swift, silent, mysterious. 'Oh, for a walk,' he would say, smiling, 'for a ride,' as he leant his bicycle against the cook-house wall. 'Just for a bicycle ride,' he would say, smiling softly. 'Why a bicycle ?' father had asked, slowly, looking up over the richly bound volumes and sheaves of fine paper on his heavy, highly polished desk. 'I thought I gave you enough for that car Sapru was going to sell you.'

'Yes,' airily, from Arjuna. 'But I prefer the bicycle. It was so much cheaper, second-hand,' and father pursed his lips, obviously refraining from questioning

131

him over the remainder of the money. 'It's so light, and no trouble,' and, to me, 'besides, one can go everywhere where one couldn't in a big car. Sapru's car !' he laughed. 'It is as big as father's—almost.' And his eyes twinkled briefly. 'But don't you mind ? In the heat ? On all those dirty streets ?' But Arjuna never minded. 'No, I don't mind,' he said, shrugging, smiling with faint cynicism, and then vanished. He never walked away, he disappeared. And perhaps that was why we forgot him so easily. When he left—that final time, for good—there was no void; he was merely absent, and one did not feel an absence, not Arjuna's whose presence itself was so half-hearted, and barely felt. Besides, he had disappeared so often before, and his reappearances were all so quiet, so unobtrusive, that all happened with a sad naturalness and one felt ashamed to question. 'He is gone,' father had said, holding the letter in his hand like an empty cage from which a bird had escaped—a bird once beloved, but for so long known that one had grown too used to it to count it beloved any more. One had pitied its sufferings. 'Gone,' I had repeated, with momentary anguish. And no one had tried to bring him back. His world had never been ours, he had merely been a visitor, and had now taken his leave.

Amongst us, he had been uncomfortable. For long he had borne it in silence, like a resigned bird, but one that still gazed with passion through the bars that held it in and, after twisting and turning about on the chair on the terrace where we all had our tea when I returned from school and he from college, he would finally rise and leap across the flowerbeds onto the drive. 'I'm going for a little walk,' he would cry, if I were alone with him, but, if father was present, not even that. Then silence. Because father would press him. 'But where ? When will you return ? Aren't you coming to the club with us ? Will you be home to dinner ?' And if Arjuna replied at all, it would be with merely a brief 'I'll be back soon.' But he would not. As a school-boy he often stayed away a night, like a domestic cat that gives way to its lust for freedom once night falls, and nothing can keep it in. Later, he would be away for longer and longer stretches—for days at a time. It was of no use trying to locate him. Father would grow quieter and quieter—I used to think with anxiety, but now I feel it was anger. Perhaps he did make enquiries—I do not know, I did not like to bother him with questions when I saw him raise his hands to his temples and frown. 'Where have you been?' he would ask, slowly, coldly, as Arjuna strolled in through the backdoor, cool, a little dirty as though he had not had a proper bath, but cool, as though he had walked in rain and dew. 'Where have you been? I should like you to give me an exact account.' At first it had seemed only right that he should ask. Later, seeing the gentleness of Arjuna's smile vanish, seeing him back up against the wall and raise his chin defensively while his lips went a little white, I wondered if it would not be wiser for father not to be quite so cold, so terse, so grim. With me, he never was, no matter what I did—even I noted the difference, and felt uncomfortable. But Arjuna would not be cornered, could not be made to give 'an exact account. 'I was staying with a friend.' 'Who is your friend ?' 'Just— someone from college,' waving his long, brown-fingered hands. 'What is his name ?' Spitefully then.

'Farid Mohammed.' A still, ferocious pause. The Mohammeds—one did not know people like the Mohammeds, but one knew that they lived in a disreputable quarter of the city where tailor-shops jostled the butchers', and people slept out on the street on string-beds at night. Badly-off, disreputable Muslims who thought nothing of spitting *pan*-juice on their walls, of allowing their daughters to wander about the streets and shops unescorted. Father's lips grew narrower, tighter, his fastidious fingers folded away the newspaper, setting it aside, as he prepared for a lengthy talk. But Arjuna would not talk, and the older he grew, the less he spoke. He would turn swiftly to run up the stairs to his room—that faraway, locked room that no one ever entered except his friends, the servants. Father would halt him. 'No,' he would call in a voice that pursued him up the stairs. 'Arjuna !' And Arjuna would lean over the banister and look down, raising an eye-brow, with a face so distant from us down below, so unrelated to our thoughts, our values, that one might as well have talked to a starfish as to him, and so there was nothing to do but set him free. Set free. If I was a partridge, plump, content, he was a wild bird, a young hawk that could not be tamed, that fought for its liberty.

'Gautama, what does it mean when you dream of the dead ? I dreamt about my mother this afternoon— about the photograph father has of her, on his desk. She is all in grey. It is such a clear photograph, but everything looked grey in my dream. What could it mean ?

'Nothing. Dreams mean nothing.'

134

Why were my only memories of Arjuna those of the distance between us? He had been a good brother, he had loved me and I him. Now, leaning back and closing my eyes, it was with an effort that I conjured up the giant, cream-billowed clouds that precede the monsoon, and saw them scud across the vast sky, and the tenuous paper kites that we sent skimming up on the strong breeze, flutter in the sunlight—some scarlet striped, others emerald green, crimson and black, canary yellow and pink ones that bobbed, curtsied, dipped and then rose, rose, rose on length upon length of fine, cut-glass-sharp thread that we held on bamboo rolls between our hands. Mine were awkward kites that never lost their earth-bound inclination. Arjuna's were birds—hawks, eagles, swallows—in the wind. 'Silly girl,' he would laugh at me, 'Get Hari to help you. Launch it for her, Hari,' and while the washerman's son helped me with mine, instructing and aiding with deft fingers, Arjuna would effortlessly manoeuvre his, which sailed high, high, together with kites and eagles that wheeled on motionless wings up and down the roller-coaster air currents. The sun would set, the clouds would be illuminated by orange and rose fireworks that exploded within them, and the trees would turn to black silhouettes that stirred with the murmurs of evening birds. 'Aren't you ever bringing yours down?' I would ask, swinging bare, mosquito-bitten legs over the parapet, for my arms were tired and the back of my neck ached. 'In a little while.' He would reply, as he fought battles with kites flown from other roofs and brought them down, one after the other, cutting their threads with his kite's, so that they quivered like wounded birds and then drifted to earth,

135

turning slowly over and over, giving the children waiting in the gardens and streets below time to make a mad scramble towards the spot where they thought they would come to rest. But Arjuna could never have enough, and, in the twilight, my old *ayah* would come toiling up the stairs, complaining of her rheumatic aches, to fetch me for my bath. 'Imagine having an *ayah* at your age !' Arjuna would snort. 'Does she bathe you too ?' (Of course she left later, soon after.) And Arjuna would remain on the roof to smoke a cigarette with Hari and talk of the football matches they went to see together.

Why had it been so easy to forget ?

'Dear Maya.' For the first time in his life he wrote or, in any manner, addressed those words to me. 'Dear Maya.' Dear sister, dear small stupid silly sweet sister, it said . . .'I heard you are married. Impossible to believe, yet it was, of course, the inevitable for you, and I am sure you are very . . .' Strange Arjuna, strange brother. That astringency that had always given an edge to his low voice, it clung to the written words. The tartness, the aloofness in them. I heard his voice again—low, swift and urgent, when he was serious, and carelessly soft when he was not, as though it did not matter whether you heard him or not. There was a river-strength in his words that no dam could ever have halted—they would simply leap over and away, their high, quick waves glistening. The letters rose high as the kites he had flown, and straight, and then flowed on almost indecipherably. How different from father's writing. But he had been different in every way. '. . .The sentimental urge of the bourgeois

136

to sit down and write to you, my first letter home.'
Strange words, as though they came from Gautama's
cynical tongue, not from my father's son's. And what
was the urge that made him write this ? Not senti-
ment, no. 'It disturbs me to think of you living still
as you did when you were ten years old, in father's
world of drinks at the club, parties on the lawn, bad-
minton, flowers and poetry.' This was not to be understood ! 'Here I work with my hands in a canning
factory. I am not paid much yet, and it is sometimes a
problem to make ends meet; but I find it exhilarating,
and it is clearer than ever to me that life, no matter
how elegantly lived, is meaningless when it is lived for
nothing but one's own pleasure . . .' Why write this
to me ? After all these years ? In this first letter home
there was nothing but denunciation, denunciation of
the sweet, prosperous, joyous life to which he had been
born, and which he had turned his back on, to sail
into a canning factory.

'What is the matter, Arjuna ? Is this not good
enough for you ?' father asked once, coming as close
to a blaze of anger as ever he did. Frozen anger, like
frost-bite. 'What do you go into those slums for ?
Why do you need to consort with butchers' sons? I
have sent you to the finest college, where you can
make *worthy* friends, and you turn to—city loafers.
Haven't I found suitable friends for you?' 'Mohammed
is my friend—and Hari.' 'Hari ? Hari ? Who is he ?'
suspiciously, rattling the newspaper, and my eyes
grew large as I hid behind a vase of poinsettias,
to listen, frightenedly. 'He lives here, on your compound, and you don't know him!' Yes, on that occasion
voices had been raised, bitterness had burst out of its
137

poison sac. 'The *dhobi's* son.' 'You are not permitted to play with the servants, or their children, you know that. I have explained to you it is not fair to them.' 'I don't understand why not.' 'If you were a gentleman you would understand without being told.' 'A gentlemen ! Damn all gentlemen, lying, cheating hypocrites, damn them all...' The first violence in our household, the first act of violence, as Arjuna flung out his arms, crying 'Damn them all,' his lips quivering, and father standing up to take him by the arm—then Arjuna escaping. Arjuna escaped.

'How I used to try and persuade you to run away, when we were children. Even the sight of the basket with its load of match-sticks and bread for the journey wouldn't persuade you. But to me it was stifling, false...I live now, not comfortably, not prosperously, but I work hard, and I know that work has meaning...'

Hard work ? Meaning ? And, Arjuna, what of our home? Our father? After all, what was his money spent on if not on the feeding and rearing of the many servants and their impossible families who lived in the quarters behind the fruit trees? And the feeding of hungry performing bears and their trainers who pulled up their shirts to rub their bare bellies? What else could one do ? There was the government, all kinds of laws, aids. And father never did wrong, Arjuna, all he did was to sometimes throw a party to which came people magnificently dressed and delightfully gay, to sniff at the roses while they sipped their drinks, and were witty and courteous and amusing, till father's guest artiste arrived. A great singer. 'The appreciation of art is graciousness itself,' father said, in Urdu, and when he pronounced those words in his
138

rich, cultivated tones, they gathered round them a perfumed load of meaning. Meaning, Arjuna searched for meaning. But I had found it long ago, as a child, in the singer's voice, as it sped effortlessly to the heights and depths of tone, a voice that was mellow rather than sweet, echoing rather than piercing issuing from the little bower at the end of the terrace where, in daytime, the pigeons came to be fed. She sang of love, unrequited, of passion dying, of wine, of lovers, of roses. What sin did Arjuna see in those masses of roses that, each winter, illuminated our garden? And once again I wandered down the trim grass-walks between them, with my father, admiring them aloud— the large pink ones with all the promise of sunrise in them, and none of sunset's brooding tints; the small, pale yellow ones, as sweet and cool as the icecream that was made for me on summer evenings, in a wooden barrel filled with crushed ice; the white ones, tight buds with petals slowly unfurling; tinged with the green of new birth; and, best of all, the red ones, so deeply red that they seemed black at their hearts, wickedly, ravishingly black. And father's silver scissors snipping off the dead heads, pointing out to me a bud of glorious peach colour, or a small honeysucker flitting over the beds. Surely no worm gnawed at their roots, no canker at their hearts. Where was their sin? Where did you find their sin?

'The stagnant dregs of a sentimentalism available only to the decadent.' Who had said that ? Arjuna ? Gautama ? It could have been either. No, it must have been Gautama who alone used words as pebbles to strike with, not, as Arjuna did, dry faggots to light fires with. 'Capable of seeing nothing but illusions,

139

imagining them to be real. Fairies in the rosebuds !
The lash of my whip.' Neither of them had seen
rosebuds where they wandered. But then, they never
wandered—they always walked with purpose. 'Where
are you going, Arjuna?' 'Oh, just for a walk.' But
that was not true, for he walked swiftly and straight
down the streets to visit his friends, or to the library.
Later he walked in processions, carrying banners that
had slogans painted on them, in red, shouting, with
white lips, scuffling through dust, perspiring. 'Quit
India,' the banners had read, and they had paraded
around Government House, outside the courts. His
name had appeared in the papers, and father saw it,
and his lips, too, went white, and he had got up from
the table where the three of us sat together, conscious
only of the sticking plaster on Arjuna's forehead, and
not of the tea-cups, and he left the room without a
word. And then Arjuna had left. And we had never
seen him again, and never spoken of him again, and
nearly forgotten him.

'. . . To return one day. Without roots, one cannot
grow to any height. . . is what I tell my Negro friends
trying to persuade them to return to Africa. . . more
useful there. . . My plans. . .'

His plans. His desk covered with papers, his shelves
with books. Cheap paperbacks, not like father's books,
leather-bound and embossed, or mine, coloured and
gay. His were so often on loan that they were grimy,
tattered, and heavily marked and scored. 'How badly
you handle your books,' I would sniff, knowing, from
father, that this was a cardinal sin, and being myself
the possessor of ivory book-marks, sandalwood book-
stands, Tagore, Keats, Shelley, *Little Women*, the

Panchatantra and the Arabian Nights—all in illustrated volumes. 'Well, I don't just look at them—I read them,' he would say pointedly. He did, late into the night, shut away from us. And now his brown fingers worked on cans of beef and pork and cabbage. His white lips, his brown fingers. Shut away from us.

But now he had tried to reach out to us, after all choosing me from his past and half-forgotten world, the damned one of flowers and garden-parties. 'Damn them! Damn them all!' he had cried, had now he worte with cynicism, 'Have you changed? One must move away, quite away from one's crib and swaddling clothes. They playpen of home... not without dangers. After all, if father did not belong to that sheep-fold of superstitious, hide-bound Brahmins, there would never have been that absurd fuss over a horoscope that, I remember, was once cast for you...the tantrums, do you remember?'

Do you remember?

'You look as though you haven't moved out of that chair since I felt you this morning. And why haven't you opened the windows yet? It's quite late.' With a crackling, spitting sound, the bamboo screen was rolled up. The sudden influx of air and dust made me realize, with a start, that the window had been flung open. The crows were squabbling in the garden, the light was the uneven colour of a ripe, peach skin, as though the afternoon sun shone out of the heart of a giant, hot palpitating fruit.

'I see you have got your letter at last. Father well? Let's have tea.'

'Father didn't write.' Oh no. Father was too busy

peeling an iced lichee in the blue dusk of the rose-scented terrace, too busy ordering long drinks for friends who had come to call—barristers, poets, professors and philosophers who came to sip drinks, to throw back their heads and speak, in gentle cultured tones, of books and gardens, art, art. . His daughter ? Ah yes, she had married and gone away. His son ? Ah yes, he, too, was away. Would they return ? He raised his beautiful manicured hands above his shoulders, shrugged, smiled. Who knows? The light fell through the convolvulus to gleam on hair that was soft snow, or silver foil, in the twilight.

'No ?' Gautama was surprised. He sat over the tea-tray, rubbing his hands. 'You look disappointed.' He looked at me, waiting. I did not move. So he shrugged, poured out his tea. Yes, it was best for him to learn how to do that himself. One of us would be left alone to always pour out his or her tea, in loneliness, and I felt the shroud of death blur my vision, while through it I saw him sitting, miles away in the distance, squeezing out a small, yellow lemon that filled the stale air with a sharp, shooting odour of astringent freshness. The limes that shaded the dog's corpse had emitted just such an odour upon a fine spring evening, long ago. Death and youth, stillness and sensation. 'Who was the letter from then ?' he asked, settling back comfortably with a cup of tea. He had had a good day in the courts, hence his excellent mood.

It embittered me further. 'Here,' I said, and flung it onto the table. I saw the long white envelope shoot out of my cove of dimness into the bell of light, and lie there on the table-top, gleaming. The horoscope, on yellow parchment, had gleamed thus in the light

142

upon my father's desk, in a very different room. It had borne with it the etiolated touch of the albino, smelt of him. It had been torn to bits.

'Who ?' Gautama asked, turning it over, puzzled. 'Arjuna ?' he frowned. 'But who is that ?' and deep lines ran from end to end of his wide forehead on which no bead of perspiration ever stood. 'Who is Arjuna ?'

I smiled. 'My brother. My long lost brother who ran away from home at the age of twenty-two and was never heard of again. He has written to me now, to tell me he is working in a canning factory in New York; and fighting the Negro cause. My brother was always the rebel—unlike me.'

Gautama's long, papier-maché face broadened out as though it was made of clay after all. 'Well,' he exclaimed. 'Well, is this not amazing. And you never heard from him in all these years ? Or spoke of him to others ? Why not to me at least ?'

'Father disowned him.'

Now that he had read the letter, Gautama began to smile. His mocking, amused, objective smile that I hated. 'Well,' he said, 'I must say this is quite amusing. Incredibly amusing. A piece of fiction. Here we have father's pet, spoilt and cosseted, and there—was he your mother's pet ? Yes ? I knew it—your brother, cast out from the bosom of the Brahmins, an outcast, a sinner...' He read out bits aloud, chuckling. 'Incredible !' he exclaimed. 'Why, this is too much like a portion of a serialized romance in a woman's magazine. Not that he lacks style—literary style. Or conviction. That, too, is certainly there. What amuses me is how this young man, barely older than you, revolted so violently against an order that you so

143

naturally gathered to your bosom as the only way of
life possible for the Brahmin daughter of a Brahmin...'

'What are you saying ?' I cried, passionately angry.
The light from the open window was too bright : it
hurt my eyes like a giant red thumb pressed into the
sockets of my eyes, and lit up Gautama's face luridly.
'What are you going on about ?'

'Why, about this priceless letter from the noncon-
formist son who shocked his family by his non-
Brahminical, even *anti*-Brahminical beliefs, one might
say. It seems to me a most amusing topic for conversation. As far as I can see, you, with your profound
interest in human beings and their variant natures,
ought to be amused too.'

'Amused ? Human beings ? What are you talking
about ? They are my brother and my father !' I
shouted, rushing to the window to let down the bamboo
screen. Once more a cloud of sulphur dust arose
from it, choking me. It might have been morning.
Gautama might never have left, the letter never arrived.
... But no, the evening light was orange, pink, the
letter opened. I had read it, I had found what so far
I had hopefully doubted—that the astrologer, the
horoscope, the 'tantrums' were not figments of an
insane nightmare, no curious hallucination, but facts,
corroborated, solid facts, remembered, known. Yes,
the evening light was orange, pink.

'Human beings all the same,' Gautama's voice ran
on. 'But of course is imposible for you to see them in
a detached light, objectively.'

'Impossible, yes !', I cried. 'Impossible ! Such
things are impossible, and I rushed away into the
bedroom, slamming the door so that the blood jolted
144

to a standstill in my veins as the bang echoed through that deathly house. As I threw myself on the chair before the dressing-table, crushing bottles and posies between my fingers, that echo was transformed into the rhythm of drumbeats that grew in strength and volume, grew and did not diminish. This is not natural, I told myself, this cannot be natural. There is something weird about me now, wherever I go, whatever I see, whatever I listen to has this unnaturalness to it. This is insanity. But who, what is insane? I myself? Or the world around me? And the vibrations of the drums quivered like ripples touched with froth across the mirror, distorting my round, plump face into a peaked, elongated one with ghostly eyes, a great, anguished mouth. I stared at it.

Presently, Gautama came in, having, no doubt, finished his tea first, and lifted my face from the dressing-table-top with one hand. 'Now what is the matter?' he said, not unkindly. 'How hot you are. I do believe you haven't washed your face all day.'

I ground my forehead slowly back and forth in the palm of his hand, ardently desiring that cooless, that flat dryness to be a part of me. But his hand did not really touch me at all, only the image of an upset child in the mirror. 'You do not understand,' I said at last, which were always my ultimate words in a conversation with him these days. 'You do not understand.'

'Perhaps you do me an injustice,' he said, in quiet tones, and I looked up into the unsteady mirror to see him move away, light a cigarette, blow a spume of smoke into the dimness. 'This is an unnatural state of human affairs, certainly'—unnatural, he used that word : it hung in the atmosphere itself—and he puffed, puffed gravely, with his pontifical air, and, indeed, he should have been a judge, I smiled in bitterness. 'But not an extraordinary or a complex one.' he went on. 'If you knew your Freud it would all be very straightforward, and then appear as merely inevitable to you—taking your childhood and upbringing into consideration. You have a very obvious father-obsession—which is also the reason why you married me, a man so much older than yourself. It is a complex that, unless you mature rapidly, you will not be able to deal with, to destroy. But then, it will probably destroy itself in the end, since passion of this sort is almost always self-consuming, having no object within its range that it can safely consume. Any little set-back destroys it, leads it closer to its termination. The delay of a letter, a long separation the realization that another person—another person very close to both you and your father, whatever you might say—does not place the same trust as you do in the adored figure—all this shakes your faith, proving it to have been—'

But here, since no lightning bolt would fall, no thunderclap break on this bleak, comfortless figure, I broke a storm loose myself, by striking out at his absurd reflection in that tall mirror, with such force, with such unconsidered force, that the great oblong of the mercurial cage went swinging backwards and upwards, bearing with it a heap of half-filled bottles of perfume, and the world was tilted upside down, insanely, unnaturally, so that our faces appeared bloated, as though they were the faces of corpses floating in a grey sea, and our limbs receded into the distance, elongated into long, undulating yellow waterweeds. It was so grotesque that I pressed my face close to the mirror, close to that bizarre reflection, and grinned into its teeth, then burst out laughing. The room was filled with heady. dizzying perfumes—rose, lily, jasmine—all those little bottles were pouring out such overwhelming doses of essence, the very furniture tottered. And Gautama, even my wise, steady, calm Gautama, fell on his face beside me, gripped my shoulders and said, as only he could have thought of saying, 'You have fever—I do believe. you have a temperature, Maya.'

I am in a fever then, and it is not a rat at all, that odoriferous creature nibbling· at its squealing mewling young, whipping them closer to its body with a long, germ-ridden tail—it is only a fever. And my father, who sits in a corner beside the mirror, so that I can see two of him and he is doubly impressive, doubly unreal, is not the one who is nibbling either. Nor is it his tail that lashes. It cannot be, for he is eternally smoothing down his silver hair with white fingers, or placing finger-tip against finger-tip to form a most inviting little cage, over the top of which he smiles at me, sweetly, crying. 'Have a lichee ! Have a lichee !' No, no. His voice is not such a squawk. That must be a peacock in the jungle outside, screeching with insane joy and fear at the sight of a rain-cloud over the horizon. 'In Italy, in Italy,' he says, smiling, tapping pink finger-tip against pink finger-tip. 'In Italy—' 'We have lichee ?' screamed the peacock, teetering upon dancing toes, the weight of its spread, many-eyed tail unbalancing it. 'No, no, Maya, they have no lichees there, child. Figs, blue figs . . .'

'Scented ?' 'Scented ? What scent ? God, what an odour ! The wind must be blowing from the crematorium today.' 'Turn it, turn it,' squeal the rat's young, and rn scampering towards the door, their furry, fleshy bodies slithering over mine as though I do not lie there, in their way, but am bodiless, a disembodied soul that drifts about in a limbo, sometimes on the floor, under the bed, sometimes up under the ceiling, from where I look down and smile to see the furniture at such odd angles. 'You do look funny, father, you do look funny from here !' 'What ? What?' and he jumps up, jumps up and down, while I sail higher and higher, farther and farther, crying, 'Higher, Arjuna, higher ! Oh, see it sail, see me sail !' And he appears smaller smaller, poor father, till he is lost in the labyrinths of the mirror.

'Arjuna !' I cried then, sitting up in a panic. 'We must find him.' 'I'll send an expedition to the African jungles.' Arjuna promised, and I heard the Kathakali drums begin to beat, Kathakali drums begin to beat.

The fever ebbed, as day ebbs, as night and sea ebb, silently, and left me sitting high and dry on the silver sands of a hot, oppressive evening, eating water-melon, biting moon-shapes into the crisp, crystalline, rose-red flesh, and spitting out the flat ebony-black seeds. The stars, too, were seed-like, not larger, and dull, choked by a pall of dust. No breeze stirred, though we sat up on the flat roof of our house, where no trees could screen it off if it came. Yet it was hot, still. The garden seemed far below, another world, and we hung upon a cloud of dust, like worn and shabby angles, looking down to see the tops of trees. There were no flowers left now, except for a few large, pale oleanders like exhausted stars fallen upon the shrubs to die. The parapet under our feet was hot, baking. The soles of my feet were puffed with heat. A cricket stirred beside me. I popped a seed at it, saying, 'If we collect them, I'm sure we could do something with them,' and finished my melon, laid down the rind, still with an inch or two of pale lettuce-green, ice-cold flesh to it, tinted with delicate pink at the top, about the tooth-marks. I fingered it, relishing it still.

'Aren't those pumpkin seeds you are thinking of?' Gautama said, picking up his third slice, 'It was a good idea bringing that melon up here on the roof. It is somewhat cooler.' He glanced at me. 'You look quite normal again,' he said, then stopped short, disconcerted, and added swiftly, too swiftly for a man who spoke always in the unhurried tones of a logician, a philosopher, 'Your temperature *is* down to normal again, isn't it?'

'Yes,' I said, drily, and began popping slippery seeds between my fingers, one by one. 'Quite normal, thank you.'

'Good. I see you have been up and about the house again this morning, haven't you?'

'Did you?'

'Yes—books put away, flowers here and there, you know.'

'Fancy your noticing. Yes, I was up all morning. I cooked a bit, and wrote some letters.'

'Ah, did you?' He ate his melon with concentration, but of course it was not the melon he was concentrating on at all.

Owls whispered softly in a tree below us. The sky

149

seemed far away, but its load of dust very low and close like an old, shabby purple cape that had lain too long amidst mothballs and mildew, and now stifled us. It was the worst of summer.

I waited. I knew he could keep no secrets, having the candour of those who view nothing subjectively, nothing with passion, and finally he asked, 'Did you ever answer Arjuna's latter?'

'Why do you hesitate to ask ?' I smiled, stretching my arms up and back, then dropping them tiredly down on the arms of the chair that enclosed me. The cane was sticky with moisture, my skin clung to it. I drummed my fingers lightly upon it, and mused, 'No, no I haven't. It would be a difficult letter to write. What am I to say ?'

'Yes, yes, I quite see,' he said, strangely and extraordinarily embarrassed. But once he had done away with that vivid, fresh fruit that had looked so ridiculously out of keeping with the blanched, nicotine-stained fingers that held it under that solemn chin, the life-saving chain of cigarettes begun upon, he relaxed again, was himself, having forgotton my fever, though I discovered, not my brother. 'It is quite a strange case after all,' he said, and when I jerked myself upright in my chair, he held up his hand, saying 'No, no, I don't mean to start on that again, not at all. But one thing does disturb me. You never explained it. What was that horoscope he wrote about ? About which there was such a to-do in your household. Why ?'

And softly, softly the drums crept across the desert, stole through the dust. Softly, softly they began to beat. Closer and closer came the sound, louder and louder. 'Ah,' I cried, looking up to see if I could

150

find. . . Nothing but the sound, irrepressible, relentless sound of drums, drums beating.

And Gautama, who sat smoking elegant wreaths of white into the violet warmth, heard nothing, saw nothing. He was blind, blind, could not and did not care to see, to hear. But then, it was better so. He must not know, not even guess. Never, never, never. If he guessed, new dangers would arise like sudden fires out of the cracked earth, and then there was no one, not even my father, to save me. Ah, if Gautama found out, would he, might he not put me in peril of my life ? Did he not love life too, its problems, their solutions, the methods of solution ? The mystery, the mystery. Soft, soft, with care now, Maya, with care.

'Gautama,' I stammered, stretching out my hands to him, without expecting him to touch them, not even desiring that touch. 'Believe me. Gautama, I—I do not remember.'

And then those fierce headaches began, frightening in their intensity, clenching in their steel jaws my entire brow, then shifting a tortuous weight to a point between my eyes—the albino astrologer had touched me, just there, had he not?—then to one side of my head, till only that seemed to exist and I became a half-headed ogre, then slipped across my scalp and down to my neck, throbbing like a drum. The drums never ceased.

'Stop them, tell them, tell them to stop,' I begged, when in this state. And then, in the convalescent calm that followed, wondered if such drums existed. In all my sane life—and surely there were times when I was no longer sane !—I had not heard such a rhythm—uneven, so that it could not be an accompaniment to a

151

dancer, or, at any rate, to no ordinary dancer, slow, yet persistent, so that they were funereal rather than festive or ominous. They sounded as though the drama was not about to begin but already over. I searched for the dancer then, the powerful dancer gone berserk, but found only shadows, for he had danced his dance, departed to dance elsewhere, leaving only the rhythm pounding in my ears.

'What to stop?' Gautama queried, looking up from his book with a face as detached as a mask.

'The drums,' I complained once, weakly, and then, in horror, was silent, for Gautama must not know. There'd be new dangers then, greater dangers. Secret, secret, all my own.

'Why not go away for a holiday?' he said that night.

'Where to?' I cried. It was all a desert, without an oasis, and I was tired of pursuing mirages.

'With your father—wherever he goes,' said Gautama, still in that unrelated, disconnected voice-from-behind-a-book—or so it sounded to me, who lived on a different level, one of tensions and perpetual thrill, and could no longer breathe in the lower, slower world that was his.

'Father,' I said, as though tasting a strange word. Then smiled in pain, for it was bitter. And yearning, suddenly, I turned away, ran, called Arjuna to find him, fetch him, but Arjuna sent me a message saying that he was searching still and father was not to be found. And then came the astrologer, bleached, opaque, flicking the cloth between his thighs, flicking, and flicking, to ask me whether he could be of service to me, and the lamp began to die, flicker and fade, so that it was in darkness that his shadow crept up on

152

me, closer and closer. I turned in desperation to find someone to help me, but no one came to ward that shadow off. For the first time in my life I was defenceless and utterly alone.

Shadows and drums, drums and shadows.

The letter came, eventually. 'The heat this year is quite unbearable,' it said, in small pale green letters written, I knew, with a silver pen that had never made a nasty scratch on that thick paper. 'Necessary to take a long holiday, a complete rest. . .I shall be sailing for Europe on the tewenty-first of May. Austria should be the most drastic change from my present surroundings . . .parhaps the Italian Alps as well, in autumn maybe Spain. . . return in winter, when I expect you and Gautama to come to me so that we may have a long. . .'

'Gautama,' I said, pressing my hands to my ears. 'Arjuna. I believe I am ill. Something has gone wrong.' But in silence only—I no longer dared speak aloud. It must be kept a secret. The danger of it, the terrible danger.

6

We walked to and fro on the platform that heaved with turbulence and unease, amidst a crowd waiting for a train to arrive and, on other platforms, crowds waiting for trains to depart. Whistles shrieked and there was a stir of disturbance, a surge of emotion— hail or farewell ? Water boiled, steam spat, foamed forth on sizzling tracks. Up and down the great staircase, across the iron bridges, great herds stampeded, and bowlegged coolies were like ants beneath great loads—not, however, theirs. 'Tea, hot tea!' wailed the vendors incessantly, and one shuffled through an armful of magazines, enticingly murmuring their alien names with a sibilant tongue. 'Melons, melons,' cried an aged crone, waving flies away from cut slices of bleeding fruit, and bluebottles rose and hummed across to cage upon cage of monkeys.

I, too, went towards them, looked at them through tears, watching them move, feverishly, desperately, in cages too small to contain their upright bodies. Some clung to the rails, staring out with glazed eyes of tragedy, at the horrible vision of hell before them, close and warm and stifling. Some whimpered, and drooping mothers cradled their young most tenderly. A few shrieked, as though they felt long pins boring through their flesh already, and revolted, and some bared their teeth in snarls of hate deeper and fiercer than any man knows. Cage upon cage of them. Long furred bodies swarming upon each other, till limbs and tails were twisted together, the elegant lines of their muscles contorted nightmarishly—the work of some fiendish maniac. And one that I saw was perfectly still and quiet, backed into a corner by the frantic bodies of its companions, and gazed out with eyes that had melted into liquid drops about to slide down its pinched, indrawn cheeks. Its brow was lined with foreboding and the suffering of a tragic calamity, and its hands, folded across its thin belly, waited to accept it. Then it spied something on the platform beside it, and, with famine swiftness, shot out one arm and picked it up, brought it close to its face for inspection, and sniffed it. It was only a monkey-nut shell, empty. A small

154

whimper broke from the animal as it dropped the shell, then was silent again, waiting.

'They are waiting for the Bombay train,' said Gautama, who stood beside me, smoking. 'They'll be piled on and taken there to be loaded onto ships for the States. They're laboratory monkeys.'

'Look,' I cried, for he had seen nothing, really. 'They are thirsty, and hungry. There's not even a bowl of water for them. And those cages!'

'Yes, there has been a lot of agitation in parliament about those cages,' he said, still smoking. 'As was to be expected, our women members of parliament have taken up the cause—'

'But look,' I begged, and he looked at me.

'You are crying,' he exclaimed, somewhat in surprise, despite the tiresome frequency of such occasions. 'It *has* upset you. Poor Maya. Here, take my handkerchief, those people are looking. Do wipe your eyes, and come, let's go and look at bookstall. No, here comes the train.'

Here it came. The great wheels ground. The long smoke spumed. Out of the compartment his mother came pouring out, so stout now that she gasped for breath as she flailed her purposeful arms, making way for her daughter and their luggage to follow. She embraced us quickly, crying out in that memorable voice that was at once soft and harsh, broken. She saw my tears. She questioned me, then went hurrying across to inspect the monkeys. She cried, 'Something must be done about it immediately', and rushed away to order water to be fetched. And Gautama said to me, tersely, 'Come on now, Maya, she'll get them water. Stop crying like that—people are looking.'

155

I ran from him, up the platform, along the train. Bits of paper with writing on them were stuck to the doors, half-torn, flapping. I studied them one by one : they bore the names of the the passengers. 'My father might have come,' I announced. 'Look for him. Help me look for him, Gautama. He'll open the cages and let them out. Hurry.' And Gautama came, took my arm, and led me into one of the cages and bolted the door behind me. There I was, amongst them, not one of those who sat quietly, in an infinity of sadness and resignation, but one of those who clung, clung to the bars till they cut into my flesh, and rattled them, shook them, crying over and over again, 'Let me out ! I want to live, Gautama, I want to live !'

Then Gautama came and took me out again, and I looked back upon the monkeys. Ah, gentle, large-hearted, small-bodied friends, send me a message now to calm me. A forest message, cool with dew and fresh with springwater. Hand me a message, a fruit. Why will you not stay? Stop, wait for me. But you, in columns of moth-warm, mother-soft grey and fawn and, sparkle-eyed, are leaving me, vanishing like mist down a jungle path, to be loaded onto the rattling vans of the Bombay Mail. Do you not know where it will lead you? Are you not afraid ? I would be, I am, as I follow you along the endless metal tracks across the desert, through the forests, towards our destiny, and we hear the train shrieking like a peacock in the void. But you move so fast, you leave me behind. You have left me, deserted. And yet I must follow, follow to the end. Lead the way then, and I'll come.

'Keep her still ! Keep her quiet ! Keep her indoors !

What nonsense you will talk, at times, Gautama,' cried his mother, flinging open the windows so that the morning sun and a bough of brazen bougainvillaeas came crashing in, and I cringed from them into a corner of my bed, resenting her entry into our tousled room before I had even dared to fully rouse myself. 'The best way to fall ill is to stay in bed,' she declared, and made me drink a cup of milk that was too hot.

'Listen to her,' said her daughter, the long-fingered, slender-necked Nila, and she helped me remove the skin from the milk. 'That is because she herself never goes to bed before twelve, and is always up at five. How does she do it ? I don't know.'

Her mother smiled at her, a smile that was like her voice—at once faraway and absent-minded, tender and involved. How much did she feel for Nila as her daughter, and how much for Nila as an unhappily married woman in need of her help? One could not tell. But she said tenderly, 'My Nila—she keeps artists' hours : sleeps all day, and, at night, when we are not there to disturb her, and are asleep in our beds, she works.' Nila winked at me, threw back her majestic head and laughed. But her mother continued, 'When you are my age, Maya, and have collected around you as many responsibilities as old people do, then you'll find five hours are all you can give to sleep, no more,' and she seemed to retreat, momentarily, into her world of trouble and suffering, hunger, unemployment, illness and helplessness. Its shadow engulfed her face, scarred it. For that brief moment, she looked twice her age, and ageless. Yet she came plunging out of it and into one of love and excitement and passion and fire, the one that her family inhabited, searching for them there,

157

to embrace them, and she turned to me that patient face and her small, broad body that was so powerful with the richness and redness of the blood that flowed so abundantly in her. If she was a figure of old age, she was as much a figure of fire and energy. The gods might one day erect a monument to her, though human beings would not. She awed me, and attracted me at the same time. Were she to lift her hands into the sky, from those gnarled tips her blood would flow in generous streams towards those who needed it. I wondered if I was one of them.

'Come now,' she cried, in that harsh voice that both irritated and impressed the very quick of one's nerves. 'Come shopping with us. We can't see Nila's lawyer before six, so we can go and buy presents for the children this morning. You have not been out since you came to the station to receive us.'

'Oh no,' I cried, shrinking from her, for if she stood for life, then she stood for the world as well. 'I can't. It is too hot. I'm quite happy here, really—'

'How can you be happy lying in bed, locked up in the house all by yourself?'

'I have my cat,' I babbled.

'Human company is what you need. Young, gay people with plenty of ideas and ambitions and occupations. We must take you back to Calcutta with us. It will do her good, won't it, Nila?'

'But in summer—'

'The summer doesn't bother one if one keeps busy.' Did she despise me a little then? My idleness? My uselessness? But she took my hand and her hand was warm. 'Come,' she said, 'Get up and come, Maya.'

And they took me out with them, and I saw again

158

the streets alive with bicycles and pedestrians, the clamorous bazaars, the Red Fort's rose-red walls swooning in dull fulvous dust, the minarets of the Jama Masjid rising like a muezzin's call to prayer into a sky of heavy, grey-tinged pearl, and people lying asleep in the shade of trees on the ghost-swept *maidan*. We went, the three of us, from shop to shop, buying, at Nila's request, the most absurd gifts for her children and their cousins, in Calcutta. Even the drowsing balloon-man was woken up, his wares bought. 'But balloons ? They'll be deflated by the time we get home,' I protested, and Gautama's mother laughed and said, 'Fill your rooms with them, then, and we'll see how long they last,' and we did the rest of our shopping with clouds of red and blue and yellow balloons gloriously bobbing behind us. 'Buy these—aren't the slippers pretty ?' Nila would ask, and her mother would cry, 'Buy them—and this sari too, they match.' And I, too, bought, frenziedly, spent all the money I had with me, and laughingly accepted their presents. They spent money like this, on fun and frivolity, perhaps once in a year, and it was to them a festive occasion, a Sunday to hardworked people. Our arms were full, we were loaded, but were too excited to stop. And in the circular park of Connaught Circus, the *gol-mohurs* still had a few billows of scarlet blossom nestling on feathery branches, so brilliant that I cried aloud, and the good women said, 'You like red ? You do ? Let me buy you these bangles then, red ones—from Jaïpur, are they ?' They spent till they had no money left to spend, and then laughed shamefacedly.

Once I had the bangles on my wrists, they drooped with their weight, and I leant against a pillar of the arcade, complaining, 'I am tired, I am so tired.' But they still had to buy gifts for Annu, and for Tuk-Tuk and for Kum-Kum, and I trailed after them, limping and yawning till my ears were filled with yawns, and I felt them, thinking they were turned to thundering sea shells. I was no longer accustomed to activity—my active mind had exhausted all my reserves long ago. Sea-shells, the sea—yes, it was as though I had been bathing too long in a high and hectic ocean. But at last they said, 'She is so tired, she will drop. We must go home now.' But then we quarrelled, for I wanted to hail a taxi, Nila wanted to lunch in a restaurant, and her mother insisted we catch a bus back, for that was the cheapest, and she was already suffering from pangs of conscience about the way she had squandered her money, though not a penny on herself, and she led us into a queue, which was no queue, but a straggling group of people tired of waiting in the blazing heat which neither *sola topees* nor wet handkerchiefs nor newspapers could ward off, and were showing varying degrees of impatience, ill temper and resignation. There we stood, waiting for the great, rumbling yellow bus that was to take us home amidst oil fumes and diesel engine roars, but the buses that came were either over full already, or going the wrong way. Even Nila wearied—like a dark swan drooping its lovely neck over a drying pond, and her mother, to rouse us, hailed the sleeping cucumber-man, and bought for us long slices of peeled cucumber, sprinkled with salt and lemon-juice, from off the trickling block of ice. Standing in the *neem* tree's mythical shade, eyes cringing at the lurid glare of noon beyond it, I bit into my cucumber, crunched it, felt it cool, refreshing, and was suddenly

revived. 'Only you would think of doing such a thing !'
I said to the old lady, filled with a longing to throw
down my parcels and embrace her—a pillar of life and
living, an anchor, much more so than her son, and the
only one I had now. Oh to live in her world, to be of
her kind ! What safety, what peace. She handed me
another cucumber, eating one herself, with relish. People
stared, and some smiled. What would father have done
—stared, smiled ? Ah, forget him then.

'People are looking !' And the dancer, too, and,
from a distance, a maniac albino. His shadow lapped me.

I drew away from the shadow, into the pool of light,
closer to those two women who had roused me, and
my home, and given us the meaning supplied by their
activities and ideas. They had not time for thinking
and imagining, little of it. Nila would sit on the floor
under the fan, and rapidly do all my sewing for me,
swearing at the darning she had to do for Gautama.
Amidst the white, starched clothes she was dark, dark
as a black swan, and as regal. Not a silent one, no, for
she liked attention too much not to reach for it, but yet
a swan, a black one, crimson-beaked. 'Nila,' I said, and
pressed her hand. She smiled, and tossed the black
hair out of her long eyes. She had come to consult
Gautama regarding her divorce. Gautama had refused,
in a noisy family conference, to have anything to do
with it. 'Why, Gautama ?' I was shocked. 'What does
she take me for—one of those two-rupee lawyers that
squat under the banyan tree outside the courts, waiting
for clients low enough to consider them—prostitutes
and petty swindlers ? I haven't time to waste on a case

like hers—the mess she makes by being too bossy and self-willed and bullying.' And in high indignation Nila had found herself another lawyer, on her own. 'You went *alone* and spoke to him ?' 'And why not ?' She was wryly amused. 'After ten years with that rabbit I married, I've learnt to do everything myself.' 'Except lead a sensible life,' said her mother, tartly, very tartly for her, for she hated this matter of a divorce in the family, and children going fatherless. But I was admiring, and 'Nila' I said, pressing her hand in wonder.

'Look at her, she's quite bright-eyed again,' said Gautama, who had come to sit with us a while that last evening before they left, with so rare a smile, I hardly believed it to be a smile. 'You have done her good, you should stay longer.'

'We would have, if you had been more helpful,' snapped Nila, with a grimace of her dark red mouth. How they quarrelled in this family, at times quite frightening me. 'As it is—what's the point ? I have to go back, the children start their exams next week, and I must look for a job.'

'And I have to go back to my creche,' said her mother, looking over a letter at me.

'No,' I cried, miserable. What, the house empty again, and I alone with my horrors and nightmares ? No ! If they stayed a while, they might help me, as my own father could not, by teaching me some of that marvellous indifference to everything that was not vital, immediate and present, I did not know how they could do this, but somehow it had to be done. They were sane people, sane, sane, and yet so much more human than my own husband. God, to be alone with him again, my unknowing, unsuspecting and steel-hard adversary in this oneiric battle, all night, all day, for how many more nights, how many more days ? God, to have to start counting them again, in utter loneliness ? 'No,' I begged, and flung myself at her knees, feeling her warmth radiate towards me. 'Stay—stay another week. There'll be a dust-storm, it'll be cooler—'

'But it isn't the heat that drives us away,' she exclaimed, touching my face with fingers that touched softly with their hard tips. 'I should be glad to stay with you a little longer, but—'

'But you shall, you must !' I cried so loudly that she was a bit shaken, and drew her hand away. Her own children teased her, consulted her, lived with her and understood her, but they did not caress her. She did not have time for caresses, very little of it, and nor did they. And yet I yearned for her to hold me to her bosom. I could not remember my own mother at all. My throat began to swell with unbearable self-pity. I would cry, I knew it, in a while, and dreaded it, in their sane presence. 'Please,' I whispered.

'How can I, child ?' she said, smiling and then frowning. 'It is impossible. But it has been nice. Why don't you go to bed now ? We shall be up early, for tea, before we leave.'

'No,' I said, 'no—' and pushed the hair nervously from my face. 'I can't—' can't enter that silent, darkened room where I should have to be alone, gazing at the shadowed ceiling, the revolving fan, with no one for company, not even a stray ray of light, for they insisted on keeping that one cavernous room dark and cool for me to rest in. Can't go out to bed in the garden, to be watched over by the moon, the ghost-white moon that sees all, forgets nothing. Can't, can't. 'Nila, talk

163

to me. Tell me about—' and I drew close as I could to the young woman and nervously began to chat, laugh. Calmly she answered. I hung upon every word of hers, every gesture, all the while watching her mother out of a corner of my eye, longing for her arms, hating her detachment. I insisted on drawing her into the conversation, away from her letters, and Gautama too, thinking that if I could but tie them all into one burning knot of contact and relationship with me, nothing, not even the fiercest fingers, would be able to extricate and banish me—or Gautama. Suddenly, I came upon that panicky after-thought, for the first time.

Trains passing in the night, I cannot bear to hear them. They all leave me behind alone.

That was an interval of sanity, of lucidity as of a bright day in the middle of the week when it is still too early to think of the coming Sunday, too late to remember the past one. And yet, remember is all I did in those intervals between the intimacies established between my guests and myself, and all I did once I was alone again. I wondered why, from the very beginning, it had never occurred to me that it might be Gautama's life that was threatened. The astrologer, that creeping, spreading sly magician of my hallucinations—no, of course they were not hallucinations. Arjuna had proved them to me, and yet—could they be real ?—had never said anything to suggest that it was I who would die young, unnaturally and violently, four years after my marriage, nothing to suggest that he even thought that. He had only emphasized that this great toll that fate would take, would be taken after my marriage, which

164

clearly shifted one half of the dancer's shadow upon my husband's head. And yet at no time did I fear for him, sense him to be in danger as, surely, I would have, if my love had been beyond the imaginary and transitory. I glanced at him now, slyly, for sly I had grown with such a load of secrets that had to be hidden from him, such evil and awful secrets. He did not look up from his papers. It was evening. He ought to have switched on the lamp, or I should have, but the muted violet shadows suited me, and he was too absorbed in a book to notice how he was straining his eyes. The papers rattled. The books emitted an odour of wisdom, delicate and subtle, but pervading, the essence of that entire study.

'Are you going to work late?' I ventured, having at length studied his long, set face, the frown which implied no greater problems than that with which the brain could deal, the thin and firm white lips, the nicotine stained hand upon which his chin rested.

He did not reply.

I switched on the light as the most drastic measure possible. And it was too drastic, for I shrank from the blow of that harsh, unshaded light with far more distaste than he did, a greater shock shattering the nerve I had so painfully summoned up. I stammered something about the time, about dinner, and left the study, letting the bamboo screen click into place behind me as I stepped out onto the verandah. I looked back to see if he were disturbed or angry, but saw him still bowed over the desk, over the book, musing, tapping his cigarette meditatively against the ink-pot mistaking it for an ash-tray, having scarcely realized that I had entered the room, had spoken, had left.

165

Could death disturb him them? What effect would the tap of the priest's faggot have, knocking against the door-post, as he came to light the cremation pyre? I could see Gautama grunting his displeasure, rapidly shaking his head to make the apparition disappear in humiliation. No, there was no mask of death upon that thinking, frowning face. But then, when I wandered into the drawing-room and once more studied myself in the mirror above the mantelpiece, there was none on mine either. It was too pert, too pampered a face, too ready to laugh, to smile. It was made for no tragedy. His face and mine—both displayed deep absorption in our lives : they were the faces of those who lived, not of those who died, or murdered.

Words tortured me now, as memories did, and Murder, that, too, followed me, relentless as a well-aimed arrow, as I passed through avenues of thought, recollection, doubt and horror. And sometimes I paused to feel the arrow of that word, Murder, sink into my flesh, and to cry, 'Is this what I have come to?'

It is the evening that breaks one's heart. At night one only hears the pieces falling.

'What is death then?' I asked, dropping down one ear-ring after the other. Two red rubies. 'What is death to you, Gautama? Do you believe it?'

'Perhaps if you clarified what *you* mean by death, I could tell you whether I believe in it or not. Though why you should give thought to such a subject mystifies me—it is definitely a new trend in you. You used to tell me you were far too immersed in your these days ? You are much too young.'

'There was a time when you would have disdained so banal a consolation.'

'There was a time when I did not need to console you with banalities.'

'One changes—grows.'

'Draws nearer to the climax?'

'Yes, death. But why a climax?'

He pondered then, for he rarely spoke without having thought carefully first. I waited, vastly irritated, and watched him unlace his shoes, with a clumsiness in those scholarly fingers that did not become them. It hurt, and I twisted in impatience, rattled rubies under my hand.

'You *do* believe in an after-life Gautama? In life unending? In the permanence of one's soul, and the resurrection of one's body, in different forms? No matter how one dies? No matter how often? Or—or *for what reason*?'

'Damnation is the bogey of the Christians. I am not, and never was, a Christian.'

'God, why must you always be so *negative*?'

'You are shouting, Maya,' he said, in shocked amazement.

I turned abruptly to the mirror, and looked down at all the bottles and instruments of titivation. I could no longer face myself, my reflection. I knew how uncontrollably my mouth jerked at times like these, when my lack of control, the dominance of fear over me, grew too obvious to others, too obvious for safety. And I let the moments pass, a long interval of time. (Time, like Murder, was an arrowhead embedded in my flesh, rusted, corroding, searing.) I was conscious

167

garden and your cat and your friends to muse upon death.'

'You remember that?'

The bitterness of my tone suddenly caught his fullest attention. 'You have grown very thoughtful,' he said, dropping down one shoe after the other. Old worn leather. 'Is this what you keep thinking about of each movement of Gautama's, but stared steadily away from him, visualizing an entire scene that I believed I had tapped the spring of now, so that the slighest undulation, the subtlest turn of atmosphere would set it into motion.

'I wish I knew,' he would say, 'why you so passionately wish to be reassured on this point. All on a sudden.' After a little afterthought, the calculating tone would continue. 'No, not so much on a sudden after all. It has been coming to this all spring. Why? What has set it off?' And his logical brain would count backwards the leaden beads on a long chain, ticking them off one by one, one as important, the other as unimportant, till he came to one, an ugly, misshapen, glinting one, and he would finger it, rolling it meditatively between thumb and forefinger, weighing it, pondering. 'Ah I have it!' So the chain would snap, so the beads would fall, scattering to the ground and, amidst a jungle clamour, roll off in a thousand directions, irretrievably. All except one which would remain in hand, and this bead he would hold up over my head, triumphantly. 'The letter Arjuna's letter! What was it that disturbed you so violently when you received it? The ruin of your confidence in your father? No. No, it wasn't that. Let me see now . . .' The long fingers would fumble,

168

the frown deepen, till the deep-set eyes would suddenly flash with illumination. 'I have it! It was Arjuna's reference to that horoscope—that strange fuss over the horoscope that was cast for you. You never did explain that to me. Why? *Why?*'

'Stop screaming, for God's sake, Maya. Maya!' And there he was, shaking me roughly by the arm, There was fear on his face as he stared down at me, holding me fiercely. 'God, what has happened to you, Maya?'

I could not look into that face that reflected my own fear, for the first time. I flung away from him, trembling. 'Don't make me tell,' I whispered, then turned swiftly to clutch at him, his garments. 'Don't ask me, Gautama—you can make me tell, you can talk me into anything. You can force me into anything you like if you just keep talking and questioning long enough. But don't drive me Gautama, don't drive me.'

'I'm not driving you,' he said, and shook me again, coldly furious. But when I cried out in panic, in a panic of pain and not insanity, he was suddenly kind, troubled—no longer afraid, but only distrubed, deeply disturbed. (Gautama, had you but caught me then, you might have stayed me!) 'I have asked you nothing,' he said, looking into my eyes. 'What do you imagine I want to force you into? What—but no, I shan't question you. Believe me, there is nothing I am trying to drive you into doing, or saying. Look up at me. Look up.'

'No!'

'Why? Why? Tell me, are you afraid of me?'

'Don't—question!' I burst out, and buried my face, childishly, into his clothes.

'No,' he said, gently. 'No more questions. Sorry, Maya. Come, lie down and rest. Take your shoes off, come on. You poor tired girl, this summer has been too much for you, hasn't it? I'm sorry my mother could not stay on longer, she did you good. Let me try and make up for it a bit. Come, I'll sit by you till you fall asleep. Should I talk to you? I'll tell you about the man who came to see me today—it's an interesting case. But wait, first I'll fetch you something to drink.'

I did not look up to see him go, but as soon as I heard his footsteps diminish in the distance, I leapt out of the bed and springing to the door, bolted it quickly. In a little while, I heard him knocking. Then banging. Then, in a fury of impatience, giving it one kick and leaving it, leaving me, in silence.

Scratch and scuttle, scratch and scuttle. Slash, slash and scream.

It had been a Sunday when we had seen them off, when the train blew one wailing whistle of farewell—a sound which, heard on a still night or out on the stretching fields of the bleak and dust-swept countryside, turns one's heart over within one, makes one raise a hand to one's mouth—to stifle a cry? To bid farewell? But, heard at the station, only made one restless, and close one's ears to its shrill, palpitating echo under the iron rafters. We came out of the station, extricated ourselves from the red-shirt coolies and luggage trolleys, and I stood waiting for Gautama

170

to back out the car, when I saw, with surprise, a bush of pink oleanders in a sooty patch of grass at the traffic-ridden gate. Pink oleanders. At home, in summer, one length of the garden wall, behind the fruit tress, was loaded with the drooping weight of oleanders, massed with bright pink blossom. Bright pink in the etherized swoon of blue twilight, bright pink again in the dew-frosted green shimmer of dawn. Yet the long arms of my memory did not stretch out towards them, but towards the single white one in a small garden outside my room, where I sat, in the evenings when father had gone out alone, trailing my hands over the arms of the chair to pick up sweet-smelling handfuls of newly mown grass that the gardener had not yet swept up. And raising that fistful of nostalgia to my nostrils, I would sigh, narrow my eyes, and look up at the new moon in the sky, sweet, fine, tremulous, and a rush of fragrance would emanate from the bush of white oleanders.

I began to dream—of my little dead dog that I had loved, of Arjuna going away in secrecy, of the pink blossoms over the wall—and long, mellifluous Sundays, white oleanders, where are you now ?

'Where are you now ?'
It is a question that crosses, vividly, my bleak mind, crosses it slowly as a tired bird struggling through the grey gauze of the evening sky. My mind is tired, I am tired. I have thought too much, remembered too much. Time ought to appear short to me now, doled out by a niggardly god, far too little of it for one who is starved for time. But, upon reflection, I find that it is not so, that it stretches, stretches

171

endlessly, and as I grope slowly down the corridor of days and nights, fearing mortally the unexpected climax, the sudden finality that lurks in some suspicious shadow on my way, I find it excruciatingly long, tortuously slow.

'Will the summer never end? Will the monsoon never come?'

'It is only May yet, Maya.'

'Only May!'

What weeks, what months must pass before that first spitting, spiteful, longed for and passionately blessed fall of rain. Rain would mean a break in the dust-choked passage of heat-struck days, it would mean a climax, of a kind. But it is only May. And I bow my head with an unendurable sense of tongue-thickening, eye-veiling depression, as I sit on my little chair and stare and stare at the only cool thing in my vicinity—the floor, its squares of soft grey and dim black and sleep white, cool, flat, serene squares of marble. One is like a piece of sky overcast by rain-clouds, and shadow swallows hurtle across it so swiftly that speed itself is transfixed and held immobile, and the birds are suspended in mid-air, in mid-marble. Another consists of dark blobs of flotsam floating on a leaden sea. A third is a window-pane, washed with streaming rain. I know them all by heart, each one of them, for I have stared at them hour upon hour upon hour, till they are sisters in a dream to me, a noon-time dream, dreamt in drugged sleep and only half-remembered in red-eyed wakefulness.

Only a dream. An illusion. Maya—my very name means nothing, is nothing but an illusion.

And when I rush to the window, or to the mirror

172

that reflects the window, I see no rain, no clouded sky, no promise, no sweetness, but only the summer heat, the summer sky, dust-clouded and sun-sodden, beneath which trees, plants, grass that was once green, now droop as though withered by lightning. The dust-winds sweep across the compound, sulphur-yellow, and drag the bougainvillaeas against the baking walls. Their thorns scratch upon the bricks. I hear them screech, sigh and sag. And I, who am nothing but an illusion, with them can do nothing but also screech, sigh and then sag.

And then again I questioned him. The nights were moonlit, and therefore sleepless—I could not rest beneath that bland white eye that watched and waited. I drew close to Gautama, begging him to console me.

'You don't speak to me.' I complained in a childish whine, pressing my body into his arms. Did he never notice it at all?

'I am so damnably busy these days, Maya, you know that,' he said, and stroked my head, lit a cigarette. 'The work piles up. I haven't closed one case, and the second is already waiting.'

'I know, I know,' I murmured, edging closer to him, farther from the moon, white white eye. 'It is too bad. We don't even have our evening walks on the lawn any more. And there's so much to talk about.'

'There does appear to be something on your mind,' and he drew away in order to look at me, enquiringly, distracted, for the moment, by my childish behaviour which, if extended too long, would soon irritate, I knew. I played upon his moods, sure in my knowledge
173

of them.

'A book I've been reading,' I lied slyly, lied even under the globe of deadly serious chastity in the night sky. 'It worries me. We spoke of death—do you remember? But what did we say? We never come to any conclusion.'

'That is not the sole purpose of logic.'

'No, no, whoever spoke of logic?' I cried. 'But doesn't it worry you too, Gautama? Are you always certain of your beliefs—their *rightness*? I am not. After all, what if we *are* wrong, we Hindus? What if there is a Christian hell? Oh, I do hate to think of it,' I babbled, crazed by fear. 'I should not like to die and find myself in purgatory, should you, Gautama? But I suppose you'd hardly notice it,' I laughed. 'Now what *would* scare you would be to suddenly find yourself in a Muslim paradise, wouldn't it? Imagine you in paradise!' I laughed shrilly shutting my eyes to the moon, hysterical.

'What on earth puts such an idea into your head, in the middle of the night?'

'You in a Muslim paradise!' I shouted. 'Can you imagine? You with all the roses and fountains and harems—harems of dancing angels, pouring out wine!'

He drew away with a jerk. His arm, his comforting arm was gone. Abruptly I fell silent, and found myself panting.

'What an absurd idea. Imagine living shoulder to shoulder with Muslims all your life, and not having a more truthful idea of their religious beliefs. Really, Maya, you are too derisive of knowledge of sound facts that can be acquired only through concentrated

174

study . . .'

Like dead leaves his words pattered down, and slowly I ceased to pant, comforted by their regularity, their sober rhythm. I drew close to him again, impulsively drew him close to me. No, I did not wish him in a Muslim paradise, no more than I wished myself in a Christian hell. Ah, the thing to do was not to die, neither he nor I, but to live, and, living, sleep. 'I want to sleep,' I whimpered, 'I want to sleep.'

But sleep was rent by the frenzied cries of peacocks pacing the rocks at night—peacocks searching for mates, pecacocks tearing themselves to bleeding shreds in the act of love, peacocks screaming with agony at the death of love. The night sky turned to a flurry of peacocks' tails, each star a staring eye.

'Can you hear them, Gautama? Do you hear them?'

'Hear what?'

The man had no contact with the world, or with me. What would it matter to him if he died and lost even the possibility of contact? What would it matter to him? It was I, I who screamed with the peacocks, screamed at the sight of the rainclouds, screamed at their disappearance, screamed in mute horror.

'Did you ever answer your brother Arjuna's letter?'

'Arjuna?' The name sounded unfamiliar. I had not thought of him for so long. The letter lay unanswered, I did not even know where. 'No,' I said, wondering at myself. 'Not yet. I had quite forgotten it.'

175

Gautama looked at me in momentary surprise. He looked as though he were about to say something, but he did not. (Had you only noticed more, Gautama, been more aware, and spoken of what you saw and sensed—the world might revolve still—coloured and alive.) I wished he had something. The last spoken word hung in the air, swelling and swelling till it became a great metal bell that dully repeated it. 'Forgotten!' The echoes rang, split into innumerable smaller echoes that sank into a rhythm, a rhythm of slow, morendo drums.

'What is wrong with me?' I cried, laughing uneasily, to break the hypnotic spell of that drumbeat. 'I forget so much!'

But Gautama had lost interest, he said nothing, and the bell caught the last phrase and rang it out slowly. 'So much!' How much? I had forgotten nothing. It was all there—the opaque eyes of the albino, the bleached hand switching the fold of cloth between the dark thighs, the oil spilling in the dark, the ants that lay drowned in it, burnt to death in the flame. I remembered the torn bits of the horoscope, my father's voice knocking out abuses in cold fury at the man who complained, whined like a brain-fever bird, then disappeared. I remembered, remembered, and how much I should have given to forget it all. What I had forgotten was the magic of my father's gentle words that had once had the power to soothe and console me. Now nothing calmed me. There was no magic that was not black. What I yearned for as the only thing that could save me from insanity, if not from the violence of an insane death, escaped me now.

Remember! tolled the bell, and the drums echoed.

softly and insidiously. Remember, remember!

But I cannot, I cannot remember. I place my face
in my hands and try to force my memory. I repeat
half-forgotten, mnemonic words from my childhood—
'It cannot be altered, you must accept.' Those are the
only words I can recall from that period, and they
pursue me. They do not enfold me in warm wings,
but with claws push me closer to the end of the long
tunnel that I must traverse. I murmur lines from songs,
whisper to myself those diamond couplets that had
sparkled in warm scented nights, here and in my
father's home. But the only one I can recall is one
that now brings tears to my eyes:

'I might, after all, have achieved the
way to grace,
Had you but granted me a few years more,
O Lord.'

I conjure up odours and temperatures out of the
air, seeking to recreate the world I have lost, and
succeed in summoning up a host of visions so vivid, so
brilliant, that they sear me and annihilate me, my
body and my surroundings, and I am torn between
two worlds—the receding one of grace, the approach-
ing one of madness. My body breaks in the battle.

Did I say that time dragged too slowly for me?
Fool! How can it be so? There is still so much left, I
have hardly lived yet. I never did learn to sing, nor to
read Persian. I never did go with my father on his
journeys, never saw the seas with him, nor the great
cities in their most becoming seasons that existed beyond the seas. Why, leave alone what I have not yet

seen, there is so much that I should like to revisit before—so many people to revisit, Arjuna, above all, Arjuna. Above all? No, that is quite false. Above all, I wish to return to my old home with its garden, its arbours and roses and azure-necked pigeons. No, not that either. Better still, my summer home in this hills, in Darjeeling, and my little knock-kneed pony that took me for rides while my father preceded me on his horse Typhoon, and the pear tree outside the bay window of my bedroom, bearing its autumn load of ripe, juice-jammed, golden fruit, and the terraces stretching out, out to the undulating line of blue hills, blue hills where rhododendrons blossom, where waterfalls spin unending skeins of white spray, chill as ice, and spotted deer roam, friendly and gentle. . . God, not to be able to go there again, to throw back my head in the mist that dewed my hair, to laugh and to prance and live the life that should not, could not ever end! Is it true then, what Gautama thinks that the world I love is fatal, and the one that is alien to me is the only one eternal?

And there was a time when even Gautama grew aware of the drums, heard their voices repeat one word they had caught and display it. Madness—that was the word he heard, Madness. 'Still sitting there? You haven't stirred out? Haven't lifted up a book, your sewing? Nothing at all? But this is madness, Maya.'

'Madness?' I screamed, leaping up at him, to strike him, stab him, have done with it, his voice and mocking body. 'How dare you? How dare you?' My outraged heart pounded against my ribs, till I choked, till I saw night about me, and began to cry hysterically.

178

(A warning : Do not take too seriously what I write now, for I cannot quite recall whether these con versations, these episodes that I relate, ever actually took place, or merely occurred to me when I sat there, alone, insane with dread. I was ill, ill.)

Will it be fire? Will it be flood?

Will the lizards rise out of the desert to come up-on us—either upon him or upon myself—with lashing tails and sliding tongues, to crush us beneath their bellies?

Will there be blood? Will there be screams?

And when? When?

All order is gone out of my life, all formality. There is no plan, no peace, nothing to keep me within the pattern of familiar, everyday living and doing that becomes those whom God means to live on earth. Thoughts come, incidents occur, then they are scattered, and disappear. Past, present, future. Truth and Untruth. They shuttle back and forth, a shifting chiaroscuro of light and shade; of blood and ashes. And I am tired of it. My body can no longer bear it, my mind has already given way. See, I am grown thin, worn. My blouses hang on me, my rings slip off my fingers. Those are no longer my eyes, nor this my mouth. I cannot bear the heaving and wearing and pounding of the frantic tide that draws itself up to me, laps me more fiercely each day. I go slowly up the stairs to the roof. and there lean over the parapet, gaze into our little garden, the gardens of others, their bungalows that are our neighbours, and search in this pattern for an order of lines and designs, a symmetry that has deserted my own life. But I have failed to

179

care for my garden for so long now, and the gardner has neglected it. The jasmine vines that were supposed to climb the walls have straggled across the empty flower-beds instead. The lawn is dying in irregular patches, yellow here, tawny there, green around the water-tap. The evening voices of birds, harsh and strident, jangle together. Which is the hoopoe's, which the dove's? And who lives in the grey house across the street? I do not know, have never visited it. Strangers surround me. The shadows of night come to hound the last daylight away. The sky is darkening. Where is the moon? Is it to be a dark night? Then tonight I might sleep, untormented by that vast luminosity, so revealing. And then soft, silver notes begin to sound, flashing up and down those piercing scales. A voice follows it. 'Sa, re, ga, ma, pa . . .' The plantains flap their long, worn leaves. It is the girls in the yellow house, at their music lesson. And I am tired of it, tired. I droop my head with all its weight, till I grow dizzy, and find myself, in a panic, staring down at the hard, death-like tiles of the terrace below, and swiftly I turn, swiftly I run. I feel my heart throbbing madly.

Why?

Wild horse, white horse, galloping up paths of stone, flying away into the distance, the wild hills. The heights, the dizzying heights of my mountains, towering, tapering, edged with cliff-edges, founded on rock. Fall, fall, gloriously fall to the bed of racing rivers, foaming seas. Horrid arms, legs, tentacles thrashing, blood flowing, eyes glazing. Storm —storm at sea, at land! Fury. Whip. Lash. Fly furiously. Danger!

180

Danger! The warning rings and echoes, from far, far,
far. Run and hide, run and hide— if you can, miserable fool! Ha, ha. Fool, fool, fool.

I am in a fever. Stop me! Silence me! Or I will fly
on, fly up, at you, through you, past you, and away.
For I am ill. I am in a fever, God, in a fever.

7

In the east the sun glared, one eye glared, so white, so
hot, that before its gaze each object, dead or alive,
cringed : the white bones on the desert shrank, split
and crumbled, and in the jungles, green leaves curled,
withered and dead. In the west hung dust-clouds,
sulphur-yellow, iodine-tinged, heavy, gloomy, loaded
with the respite that comes before storm, violence,
murder. Between the two, between east and west,
below them, the earth fell silent. So great a hush
descended, that each ear—snail's, lion's, shark's—was
tuned to its reverberating echo, listening, listening for
that final, awful crash, which might not sound louder
than the barest whimper. We were as in a gigantic
bubble, only it was not so gigantic after all—it was
slowly compressing, concentrating, squeezing, and we
waited, breathlessly, for that high moment when east
would clash into west, when sun would explode cloud.
The world grew smaller. It shrank, shrank soundlessly.

As in a chamber in which each pin-pointed air-hole
is being sealed, the heat grew. It was terrific. Standing
at the closed window, but not too close for the glass
window-pane had power to burn, the split wooden

frame to scorch, not to speak of the livid metal hasp. I could not feel any effect of the whispering turn of the electric fan at all. The hair on my neck was glued to the skin with perspiration. No breeze lifted the smallest strand, though I could hear the fan, an old one, ticking, ticking, metallically. Machinery. The only thing that might continue to tick, for a while, a brief while, before it was shattered. On the walls the lizards were still. They might well have been dead, with the open eyes of those who have sighted the ultimate. But no, if they were, they would surely fall. And in no time would hosts of minute, silent ants appear, columns of them, marching on hushed, hurrying feet, and eat away the fast-rotting flesh till only the fine white bones lay exposed to the fire. Sickened, I shut my eyes, but tenuous eye-lids were no protection against the leer of the sun that morning. The light merely turned red, tinged with my own blood that crept through the hair-fine veins across my lids. I saw the world through my own blood that morning, and it was red.

But how long could one stand with one's eyes shut, waiting? For all the while the heat was oozing into the room, pouring in like thick, warm oil, swelling and expanding till it became physical, a presence that pressed against one's body, strangled one in great, virulent arms, was inescapable. Inescapable! And my eyes were open again, staring.

But no, nothing had altered. How could it? The garden and, beyond it, the street, lay spread out, pinioned by the sun, like a great pressed flower, pressed so long ago that it was now quite sapless, dry, fading fast to assume the colour and, finally, the nature

182

of dust. Nothing could move. No leaf could stir, no blade of grass. The homely insects, the birds, bees, worms of the garden, where were they all ? They had crept away, under the bushes, under the shrubs, into the trees, into the earth, their heads bowed, their eyes shut. They might well be dead, of sun-stroke. And yet, in the neck of the lizard spanned above me on the ceiling, its pulse throbbed, and seemed a giant pulse for so small a creature, beating furiously as though it were holding its breath till its blood boiled. And then, in the very height of stillness, its tail switched. One small, brief twitch. But I saw it, and immediately a thousand rats twitched their tails—long, grey, germ-ridden. Just once, before they were still again, stiff. But it was enough. It was evil. Anger lurked in that gesture, defiance. A growing restlessness that could explode to violence.

I moved away·from the window then. I tried to do something, but when I picked up a shirt with its buttons missing, it seemed pointless, at such a time, to busy oneself with sewing on a small, blank shell button. Papers, books, all were pointless, empty of meaning, as though the heat had blazed meaning away from each word, left the letters bare, stark, charred sticks in a calcine desert, soon to crumble and be destroyed. I put them away, and wandered from room to room, window to window, and each time I looked out, blinking at the violence of the glare, the clouds had edged higher it was faintly darker, by merely the suggestion of a shade. This gradually fading light painted the vision beyond the window and so, by reflection, myself and my shell, in varying tones, darkening—harsh yellow to strident sulphur, strident

183

sulphur to bitter ochre. And then, as the darkness grew, from olive haze to camouflage khaki, from khaki to dull, purulent purple. Hot, harsh colours, like a vulture's impatient screams. Unreal colours, in an unreal obmutescence. A world no longer in control of itself. A force existing in another sphere had taken it over, was altering it into something fierce, strange, lurid, a macabre cartoon with which to frighten those innocent and, more so, infinitely more so, those guilty.

It became more and more difficult to continue my restless pursuit of window after window. The heat expanded, the bubble shrank. The pressure was tremendous, suffocating. My feet dragged and my body pushed against the resistant atmosphere, as though I were wading. Wading out of my depth. It was all strange, deathly strange. Innocence turning to guilt. Lilac to purple. Ochre to ugliness. Step by step. All silently. In utter, persistent silence. And the heat struck my forehead, settled there like an iron mask that had been fitted to me and was secured to me with instructions not to touch, by no means to remove. For how could I remove it? How could I dare. I was afraid.

Storms I had known before. Rain storms, thunderstorms, dust-storms. Matters of lightning, of sweeping winds, of fury followed by serenity. But this waiting—this long, long waiting with not a rumble of thunder, not a whirl of wind to mark the beginning of the end.

And it was the end that I waited for. The beginning had begun long ago, was even forgotten. It was the end, the ultimate, the final vision of the final fate that had to appear now—*had* to appear now. I had

184

waited too long—another day would be one too many. And in a camera of insanity, I saw a future insanity projected before me, beyond the window in a world where guilt, sin, crime, punishment all stood stock still, struck into threatening immobility by a ruthless force of fate. Dust cloaked us all, my vision, myself staring, dust and ashes shrouded us.

The lizards, with glazed eyes, glared sullenly. The tail no longer twitched, but it had done so once. That was the warning, the threat. The low clouds lowering, the strange light altering, shade by shade, drove me down a long corridor in which windows grew more and more infrequent, till there were none left at all, and darkness was the inevitable, the only physical matter left, thick and black and full of presences, a well of it. The edge of the well was slimy, wet and hideous, but a well must have an edge and he who enters a well must touch the edge. The well had to be entered. This much I knew. But in the well—what? *What*?

I gave up my haunting of the windows. Not even a ghost was left there, for the innocents in the flowers to see. The familiar wicker chair again, the support of the palm for my forehead, the slow acquaintance with darkness by keeping one's eyes shut, desperately. If only I could discover now what I had pursued so long along roads of treacherous memory, of great love, of great despair, for I loved too much, too many. Loved? Was attached, a tart, astringent voice corrected me, *attached*. The word shot down the long black vacuum and struck the very bottom of the well. Rang there, stonily. Was silent. Then the echo rose, spread, in slow ripples, and struck the sides, resoundingly. Once

185

again that word rang in my mind, clear as a drum-beat on a waiting night. Yes, so it was, I felt myself respond, clenching a perspiring hand. This was the truth, the essence of the matter, as the wise, ancient Sanskrit verses had warned me, so long ago. As Gautama's dry, toneless voice had warned me, also very long ago. It was a chain of attachment, not fate, that hauled me, slowly and steadily, down the dark corridor to the pit where knowledge lay. No apple—no sweet, crisp-skinned, sun-tinged fruit with bees sucking at its honey, but knowledge, stark, hard and ultimate as the rock-botton of a dry well.

There was no further sound. Only the memory of the echo lingered to fill and fill the room till it, together with the heat, the dust, grew unbearable. I rose from my chair, pushed at it, forced it backwards, but that only meant that more would descend from above, more would heave from the back. An escape ? No, the air-holes were sealed now. The outside world had already been strangulated, lay abused, distressed, trampled into unfamiliar, strange flatness by the low yellow dust, the high white heat.

I had no breath left any longer, to question or reply. All I could do was gasp for breath, and that made the process more and more difficult. Take a deep breath, count ten, they tell those about to dive into deep oceans and those about to be executed. But when I did so, and came to the end of the count, I found I had been cheated for it only brought me to the end of my resources, and I was left breathless. In fury, I rushed—I think I rushed—at the wall, some wall, flung myself upon it, and it was hard, cruel. But it was the end. It had come. And I beat my hand

186

against it, shouting, 'Attachment ! Maya ! Traitor !'
And immediately there rushed over me a great sweeping multitude with hurrying, hurrying sounds—hosts following hosts, tearing across in a great wind that we, in the north, call the summer *loo*.

'Dust-storm ! Dust-storm !'

The servants ran shouting through the rooms, wildly excited, looking with the alarmed eyes of the summer-somnolent shocked into wakefulness, to see if any window or door had been left open, or were now thrust open to admit the rush of stinging dust. They carried long bamboo poles in their hands with which to bang shut the ventilators high up under the ceiling which had not, after all, crashed down upon us but was kept aloft by the hard-muscled arms of the dust-heavy, heat-heavy air. The servants were quick—they had experience. Quicker was the storm—vaster in experience. Such storms had blown since the time when the earth was desert and no living thing, no creeping, crawling beasts, plants or cells stirred upon that great plain. Such storms would sweep the earth and erase the last traces of these huge masses of creeping, crawling, toiling, struggling cell-conglomerations that now wracked the earth. When the time came for annihilation.

Had it come ? I ran to the window, the balls of my feet turned to truckles. No, this was a beginning and not an end. Storm. Motion. Speed. Living. I beat upon the window as the dancer, waiting to go on stage, pounds the earth with uncontrollable feet once the hypnotic drumming begins. What agony in ecstasy, what pain in magnificence. I moaned luxuriously,

straining my body towards that maniac motion, ho
and furious, coming cloud upon cloud upon cloud,
obliterating vision, obliterating, for that period, life—
the life of dying things, of drooping plants, of screaming trees, making room for the truly eternal that would
emerge thereafter. I moaned with pity for having
missed the splendid beginning, the tingling thrill of
seeing it creep across the landscape, blotting out
houses, trees, gate-posts, a forgotten bucket stranded
upon the lawn that sent out one desperate flash, blinding, then went out and was lost, finally engulfing our
own house, my own soul.

Now I stood in the midst of it, I exulted, and
raised my arms to return its impassioned embrace.
If the closed windows protected me from its whiplash
and scorpion-sting, it still allowed me the sensation of
standing waistdeep, feet-first in the centre of the
churning broil, of having plunged with grabbing
hands and rapacious teeth into the heart of a gigantic
melon, ruby-red, juice-jammed and womb-warm from
its baking sand-bed. Red, red, ruby-red was the dust—
as though I were looking at it through lowered lids.
But no, my eyes were open, wide. I was gazing
through scarlet-coloured glasses that were occasionally
rose-red, and ranged freely from nicotine-yellow to
iodine-brown as well, and from burnt orange to livid
pink, like one's most private flesh laid bare. The time
of faded flowers, of strangled lives, of parched vision,
of hesitation and despair was over. Here was a turmoil,
a wild chiaroscuro of oven-hot colours that churned
over and over in a heat-swelled bubble around me. It
revolved around *me*, about *me*, it was mine, mine, this
life was mine.

188

Gasping, I strained to join and embrace it. Did the trees stand still? Or were they turned upside-down and topsy-turvy, pompous roots still waving in the air? I could not see, and the frenzied bougainvillaeas lashed against the window-panes, writhed and lashed, and vulgar purple blossoms by the hundred came to grief, were ripped away, lost to sight and creeper. And then the dust came pouring in, and more and more followed, and I could see nothing but its strange, tinted glow, though I could hear the trees bend, creaking and screaming in the wind that tore at them and carried away their dry, broken branches as it carried away umbrellas, thatch-roofs in a seething mass of stinging, ant-sharp grains of red-hot sand.

Here was a carnival to enjoy, merry-go-rounds and roller-coasters, brass-bands, fried-food stalls, cavorting clowns. Giggling, I rushed from window to window, beating upon them as though to beat them open. I did not need to do so for the dust steeped in through the barest cracks, and the furniture was already covered with a thickening layer of gritty, grey-white sand. It was suffocating, yes, for the heavy curtains, the unnecessary cushions, the foolish bric-a-brac, all held and smothered the dust in their dark folds, so that the house reeked of it, as a vast, sombre, bat-festooned tomb, and the odour in my nostrils had intimations of burial. Oh, to send the whole card-house toppling with one high-flying kick and swoop of arms, to let the wild wind howl down and across it leaving a great space of light and freedom in which to dance round and round, round and round. . . And I ran to the next window and breathed deeply when I saw the rush and whirl outside continuing with tireless spirits, for it gave me a sensation of flying, of being lifted off the earth and into the sunset, release from bondage, release from fate, from death and dreariness and unwanted dreams. Release and liberty. Ah, storm, storm, wonderful, infidel storm, blow, blow! I cried, and ran on and on, from room to room, laughing as maniacs laugh once the world gives them up and surrenders them to their freedom. A bit hysterically, a bit in fear, for the unnatural light in the room changed from tone to tone as though I were on a stage where the multifarious stage-lights slowly revolved, flooding me in their variant shades, now high-lighting my flying hair, now my long white fingernails, then the curious quick jerk my neck and shoulders, then the expanded whites of my eyes. Frightened? No! I ran from the thought, laughing. Oh no, what need for fright? It is relief, I called back to the gods who mocked in the dark wings, it is only relief at having survived, at having regained the will and the decision to survive. It is only relief. I promise you, you shall see—I swear—survive. . .

But then I found myself suddenly exhausted, so weary that my body was as limp as a battered tree by the time the storm abated, and layer after layer of dust settled or disappeared to reveal first the tangled vines that hung, half-dead, at the windows and the verandah-posts, then the low shrubs lining the verandah, the edge of the lawn, the trees at the far end and, finally, the high garden-wall. The wind had dropped. It dragged a tired flurry of debris up the drive, whimperingly, then ceased. The trees sagged, punch-drunk after all this bullying and battering. There was a great stillness, of exhaustion and peace, and then it

190

was broken, blasphemously, by a band of mynas that now shrieked across the garden in shrill tones of canary-yellow and victory. With an effort I threw open the window. The air that rushed in was cool, fresh, wiped of dust and heat and with a touch of water, rain and spring water, in its coolness. I gulped it as though a tumbler of water from a mountain-spring had been released by heaven for my sole benefit and ran to the door, pushed it open and hurried out onto the sunburnt lawn just as a few hard and cold bullet-shots of rain pelted down, pocked the grey dust into little round pills that swiftly dried and crumbled, for, once more, the sun came out. It was afternoon.

It was a strange evening—the atmosphere was stilled, that is why. The wind had dropped, tired of storming, there were no more flurries of dust, no whirling dervishes of burnt leaves and bones. Perhaps tomorrow it would be resumed, but today it was peaceful, still. The light on the lawn, where I had insisted on their bringing out the tea, hoping to have Gautama come early and join me and the sparrows under the limes, the light on the lawn lay like smooth varnish, painted over by the huge, swift strokes of warm blue shadows that spilt out from under the over-hanging trees and the distant house where they had not yet lit the lamps. This shifting pattern of light and shadow which expanded here, shrank there, turned the garden into a hazy, mobile chess-board; the proportions altered so that corners were obliterated and new divisions and marking-lines were formed. It took on an unfamiliar air, and yet the sparrows chirped companionably, as I sent handfuls of crumbs

191

flying through the air to them, chirped gratefully, graciously, like a gathering of polite, if vociferous, old women in brown, friendly and every-day as bits of burnt bread. I was happy to have them there, with the evening light so strangely pink, so deeply rose, flushing the grey walls of the old house till it seemed to stir with an inner life, high-lighting the tangles of bougainvillaea, tattered but brilliant and vulgar still. How each object, each nuance in the air stirred that evening! How ·richly each colour gleamed before wild shadows swamped them, and then they moved and breathed gently but audibly. It was the sort of colour scheme that Arjuna, as a boy, would have mocked at had I, as a girl, extolled it, glowingly. 'Pink sunsets and golden sails,' he would have laughed, and I would have cried, 'But it is so, it is so—the sunset *is* pink,' and it would have grown pinker and, in defiance, still pinker to my determined eyes, as I made each subtle shadow turn to glaring obviousness in order to please my hunger for the real, the close and the living.

And my thought of Arjuna brought a faint tinge of nostalgia to the evening air. The first glimpse of on-coming night. My brother. I felt the words of possession and relation upon my tongue, sweet, warm, penetrating, and then, of course, thought of my father next—and his last three letters left unanswered somewhere inside the greying house. His hair gleamed silver, silken, in those blue shadows beyond my reach, and I raised my hand in a gesture of farewell. A farewell that had been left unsaid till this evening, so perfect for calm partings and painless separations. The kites that circled high in the sky that paled, paled steadily to shades of pearl and opal, shrilled piercingly the announcement of departure. Sharp and high, those cries rang through the clear air and fell like arrows in search of set destinations. But they had no note of regret. And I, too, regretted nothing, but settled luxuriously back in the chair, sighing and bidding my father good-bye, good-bye. But his ship had sailed long ago, it was not even in view any longer, and, since it had already reached other shores, there was no reason to cry, to sentimentalize, or to sorrow. Departure, parting—they were relative things, and, to me who was to stay, mattered nothing at all on this still, iridescent evening after the storm. What really mattered? But I was too lazy to think of a reply, Gautama could do that for me. After all, I smiled, I don't have to think—I *know*, and I bent to pluck a handful of grass. The blades pricked the cup of my hand, and I sniffed them, hoping to meet once more the sweet, honey-and-milk fragrance I remembered belonged to the grass of my home, to the small garden that was my own. But no, this grass was burnt, arid, dry. Being sapless, it was odourless. I let it fall. Even odours change, vary. Ah, it is all relative, relative—why worry, then? I sank back in my chair, sighing and smiling, utterly at peace.

Even time passed with my barely noticing its passage, and it was only when Gautama did, at last, arrive, that I realized it was nearly dark, that velvet shadows had stretched out like indolent cats, rolled over and filled the softly lit garden with their violet fur and only the western horizon was still alight with summer heat and noon. I laughed to think that I had even ceased to trouble myself over the time of his return, his lateness, and then forgot to jump up and greet him. It was only when I realized that there was not a trace of surprise on his face that it came to me that he was unmoved even by my strange behaviour today—for surely it was unusual. But it did not hurt me that he showed no surprise—his preoccupation, his distance from me was a part of the pattern that I had, at last, accepted. I smiled at him, at peace with him.

'Tea ?'

Yes, he wanted tea.

Only after he had taken the cup from my hand, did he seem to realize he was now at home. He looked so startled; so like an antic owl from whose beak its prey has been snatched, that I whooped with laughter.

'What is it?' he asked, slightly put off, rather grumpy, and stirred his tea briefly.

'It's evening,' I told him, almost singing. 'You're home, and work's over for the day, you know.'

'Yes, thank God. I can do with a cup of tea and a cold shower and some rest,' he said, drawing his eyebrows together with the pain of a headache such as those that wracked him whenever he was over-worked.

I longed to question him about it, to touch his temples and soothe the pain, with caresses and words. But, of course, did not do so, could not dream of doing so. And yet the alienation, the strain of remaining aloof, did not hurt. This was as it had to be. 'Poor Gautama,' I murmured, and with murmuring that was content. 'At least it's cooler now,' I consoled. 'After that storm.'

'Cooler? What are you talking about? What storm?' he snapped.

Earlier, in another season, I would have been dismayed. My mouth would have fallen open. 'But how could you not have noticed?' I should have cried. '*How*?' And mimicking myself thus, in a secret mirror, I nearly giggled at the absurd image. All that I felt now at his surprise was resignation and even relief. It had only underlined an unawareness, a half-deadness to the living world, which helped and strengthened me by justifying my unspoken decision. It was what I had expected, and he had come home and dropped it in my lap for the asking. Guile had no room in the slow, complex working of his dry brain.

'Oh, there was a most tremendous storm,' I cried. 'For nearly an hour—or even more, perhaps. It rained too—just a few drops, but, anyway, it means the night will be cooler.' Here I bit my words off abruptly, having strayed too far. The present, I reminded myself fiercely, the present and not the future.

'Was there? I was in the courts all day—it's so stuffy and dark in there, heaven knows when the new courts will be completed, and if they'll be any better. I doubt it.'

'They look so hideously new, don't they? I like the old ones, and the trees and bicycle stands.'

'What trees?' He jumped in again, feet first, and did not notice the pit in which he fell, the widening of my eyes, but began to talk of a case that was dragging on and on. 'It's that damned defence lawyer,' he complained. 'Krishnan—he'll go far, he's so unscrupulous, he would try and bribe the prosecutor to win him over on the quiet—and probably succeed too. . .' I ceased to listen, and let him continue, filled his cup, watched him without ceasing to look at the parrots

195

that flew over his head, the slow-motion alterations in
the saffron and rose of the flagrant sky. When he fell
silent, I smiled in encouragement, reminded myself to
remain in control, was relieved to notice that he did
not pay any attention to my smiles, the quick laugther
that I had, with an effort, to suppress. This evening
underlined so significantly the the vast difference
between us, between our worlds and our destinies. It
was all so clear. He rose and stretched at last, and from
my squatting position, I saw him unfold and rise into
the sky, taper-thin, long-boned, austere, like a streak of
smoke rising from an invisible fire into a real one further
away. His tired, drawn face against that riotous sky
was so ill-adjusted, so very out of place, that it was a
miracle that one could cast light on the other, the
other throw a shadow upon the one. There was no relation at all. His shoulders sagged, into their customary
stoop, and the trees that soared upwards and outwards
with plunging vitality drew shuddering away from him,
this lean, sad figure of a weary man. Poor man. Poor
Gautama. My husband. I spoke these words in order
to stop staring, to make myself feel something for him.
Gautama, my husband. I rose and went up to him,
beginning to feel as tenderly solicitous towards him as
towards a departing guest who might never be encoun-
tered again, and I strolled with him slowly across
the lawn, feeling that an unreal ghost stalked beside
me—a body without a heart, a heart without a body—
what was he ? An unfair question, oh, grossly unfair, I
chided myself immediately. He was a tired man, worn
out by a day's hard, concentrated work. Age surrounded him, weariness steeped his limps. Grey, grey, all
was grey for Gautama, who lived so narrowly, so

shallowly, And I felt sorry, infinitely sorry for him, for this slow, harmless, guileless being who walked the fresh grass and did not know he touched it.

We passed the group of lime trees. The season for their flowering was over, but a few tenacious, ivory-tinged flowers clung to them still, and they and the thick, glossy leaves emitted a ghost of that poignant, saddening fragrance that followed me down the long and twisted passage from the point where a dead dog, a beloved pet had lain under them, its sweet flesh slowly rotting and the odour of the rot mingling with this grave-side fragrance. The remembrance came flooding across, sweet, sharp and strong, penetrating as the sour, biting scent of a lime-leaf crushed between one's fingers. I paused, brought to a halt by the memory that had suddenly stepped out and stood in my way, a beckoning figure in white. It was not only the memory of a dead dog, of its dying, but of Gautama, in a rare mood to comfort—this same man who walked beside me like a disembodied spirit clothed in off-white and a frayed tie, quite different then, raising a calm, gentle face to a sky exploding with stars and quoting, in a soft voice, so rare, a couplet that rang with sympathy and was deepened by an under-current of love that surfaced only briefly, but brilliantly. The trembling exaltation of that dragon-fly moment, that breathles poising upon a tenuous moment, so fine, so frail that the faintest breath could destroy it. And I held my breath again.

He paused, waiting for me to catch up. I followed him, said softly, 'It seems such a long time since Toto died. I don't know why—whenever I see those lime trees—I miss him, so much.'

It was not an easy confession. Gautama was not a man to whom confessions of the heart could easily be made—of the mind, yes, readily, as soon as the idea had formed, sifted and settled into coherence. But of the heart—no, it was of no use. And yet that night he *had* responded, and the memory of that response was so strong that it had forced the words from me. Having offered the confession, I was overcome with a desperate timidity, begging him once more to answer, to come and meet me half-way, in my own world, not merely demand of me, brusquely, to join me in his which, however safe, was so very drab and no longer offered me security.

Had he done so, all might have been quite different.

But he did not. Less than that, he retreated to the outposts of his flat civilization and asked, vaguely, half-interestedly, 'Toto ? Who was that ?'

The words were as grim as any death sentence, absolute and unredeemable.

It took me a long time to gather myself, to thrust aside the hurt he had dealt, and to harden to it. A biting answer formed itself on my tongue, and I thought it over with care, to render it more deadly, for, to Gautama, it was only silent thought that laid weight to anything. But by the time I was prepared, I saw he had already forgotton and wandering off along his dusty, exhausting highroad, had already outstripped me.

'The whole spring's gone by with this case still dangling,' he muttered. 'Exactly how long is it since...' Then he stopped at the verandah steps, suddenly more animated. 'I must phone Krishnan about something,

Maya—go and turn on my bath, will you ?'

I did so, and with so much bitterness in my mind that it poisoned my body and made me drag through the motions with pain. I went through the window, opening the windows and drawing the curtains, to the bathroom and there turned on the tap, It gurgled in hesitation, then spat, and the water came burbling out, laughing at my surprise. I held my hands under it, and found it cool, soothing as it splashed upon the taut brown skin and fell in sparkles to the white enamel. The wonder of running water—not that of a spring, true, not of a vast meandering river, but water all the same, moving and flowing, I plugged the tub and watched it fill, my buoyancy rising rapidly with the level of the clear water, so that when I heard Gautama come into the bedroom, I called to him, then went out, my hands dripping. He was pulling his tie off and knotting it ferociously in the process. I watched and laughed.

'What makes you laugh ?' he asked in annoyance, and grimaced at himself in the mirror. 'The sight of the helpless male, I presume. A gibbon would be defter, I admit.'

'Oh, a gibbon is far, far defter—he is the most graceful of all apes. Haven't you seen one, swinging on a tree, like a trapeze artist—only much more elegant and at ease?' The Lucknow Zoo, the *gol-mohurs* in blood-red bloom, father, fountains, flowers, fun everlasting. The sun blinded,

'No, I haven't. My education, you see, was restricted to what could be imparted within the brief confines of a small, airless, chalky class-room in a far from fashionable school. Economy demanded that,

199

and trips to the zoo with bags of pea-nuts were as far from it as elephant rides in a jungle.'

'Oh, education,' I murmured, sitting down on the bed and watching him prepare for his bath. His anaemic skin stretched on the downward, curving bones of his cage-like ribs, his prominent shoulder-blades made me pity his thinness, his appearance of being so flimsily attached to a world of solids and riches, so ill-defended against it—that is, physically. His detachment was armour enough—forbidding armour, I knew. But at the moment he had little of it, so seriously was he employed in the the strenuous task of getting out of his clothes. His clumsiness his way of attracting one impediment after another, of somehow stumbling through them, reduced him to an impatient child, and I was gently amused. 'You *are* bad at doing anything with your hands, Gautama.'

'Am I ?' he said and stalked off to the bathroom where the luscious water was falling, falling. 'Men don't have as much practice as you do. It is a question of time and occupation.' I heard him splash in, with vigour, and continue loudly, 'Now if you were to find something to do that would take your mind off the suitability of your appearance. . .' When I could make out any words above the sound of splashing, I replied, and though it was he who luxuriously surrounded himself with the cool water, running, rising, rippling and fluting, his level, dehydrated voice assured me that he was far less in contact with it than I who was removed to a distance and merely listened to it, with longing, and listened to him with something of pity, and something of regret for the great passage that always had and still existed between us, like an unpassable desert.

But do not persume, no one must presume, that our marriage was an empty one, a failure. Nor that Gautama was no more than a figure of granite to me, a mound of books that smelt faintly of mouldy rice and wisdom. For he was more, so much more. I will not say that it was he who turned an immobile organ into a pulsing heart, for that had been done long ago, at my birth, by a man who stroked a lock of hair upon my forehead and called it a feather; by four mandarin orange trees on which the golden globules of fruit glowed amidst glossy foliage as in an alien song; by the tug of a paper kite that the wind bore out of my hands and lifted into the clouds; the mellifluous richness of a Persian couplet sung in a voice hoarse with emotion, upon a summer night. . .But it was Gautama who found many more things to teach that heart, new, strange and painful things. He taught it pain, for there were countless nights when I had been tortured by a humiliating sense of neglect, of loneliness, of desperation that would not have existed had I not loved him so, had he not meant so much. He taught it the will to reflect as well, and, like a wild beast on a leash, it would strain and strain in fury till tiredness set in and, in the dark, I could say, 'He is right, and I was wrong.' He enlarged it, so that many new experiences could come within its compass, and it grew greater. Heavier, too, of course, so that at times I felt it to be a load, and stormed, 'Why should I love him? I wish I did not!' But then, what is it there for if not to feel sorrow? There never lived a bird that did not know a storm, a stone, a wound. And I, an adult, thinking woman, had no more right to happiness than I had been taught, by Gautama, to regard as a privilege.

And so there was gratitude amidst all my other feelings when I turned and saw him come back, pulling a fine white muslin shirt over his bathed body, his face set in a frame that was remote, reflective and yet, not without a tenderness that come from relaxation.

Tenderness. At that moment, I felt it for him, deeply, in a rush. This, too, he had taught me.

(And yes, now that I remember, all the while I thought of him and of our marriage as things of the past. I thought of the past with regret, deep, twilit, hopeless regret.)

We went into the drawing-room, asleep already in our quiet, ever unclamorous house, except where a single lamp cast a subdued light in a ring upon the floor and the gilt lettering of dust-shrouded books. We moved slowly, and I was deeply sweetly conscious of that fresh, relaxed body beside me, turning from me now, to the radio. 'Shall we listen in to this concert you were talking about this morning?' he asked, in the brusque voice of one prepared for whatever may come next. And so I stood about, restlessly, while he fiddled and fiddled, with those meticulous fingers, picking sound like threads from the twilight, now a white one, now gold, and then merely harsh brass. But it was never the right one and then he remembered that the concert was not to begin till nine o'clock. 'We'll listen to it after dinner, then, he said, lighting a cigarette instead, and I echoed his words. but without his decision. Only with a pensive questioning to it, a sense of hard fate. He glanced at me and said. 'Shall we go out then? The chairs are still out on the lawn.

'No!' I cried, springing into action, springing to keep him from turning into the garden. 'Gautama, let us go up on the roof instead. Shall we?' My voice was loud, animated. 'It—it'll be cooler there and we haven't been there—for some time. Come.'

'Very well,' he said, indulgently, narrowing his eyes at me through the white cigarette haze with an almost loving amusement in them, as though to say, 'Anything to keep the child quiet.'

Having achieved this, my excitement which had risen, stammering, to a hot, perspiring peak, now subsided into that quiet, tender mood again through which my body seemed to glide effortlessly, and I led him out towards the verandah from where a flight of steep cement stairs led up to the roof. But just before passing out of the room, I caught sight of the bronze Shiva, dancing just a shade outside the ring of lamplight, so that the gleam of its outflung limbs and the circle of flames was steady, fixed. And yet there was nothing frozen or immobile in this pose of eternal creative movement. The powerful, slightly bent leg and the firm rooting of the graceful foot upon the squirming body of evil, and the raised leg with its arched foot, raised into a symbol of liberation, seemed more than ever to pulse with the flow of blood in them. The wise, remote face had retreated into the shadows, but its expression spoke as clearly as light to me, and I murmured a suddenly remembered passage to myself, smiling to think that my rag-picking memory had retained this scrap, without knowing from where it had wandered in, and now suddenly bobbed up on this day that had dragged through near annihilation to supreme aliveness. 'Calling by the beat of the drum all persons engrossed in worldly affairs, the kind-hearted One who destroys all fear of the meek and gives them reassurance, and points by his hand to his upraised lotus foot as the refuge of salvation and also carries the fire and who dances in the universe, let that Lord of the Dance protect us...' The sonorous Sanskrit syllables rang richly in my mind, and I was triumphantly proud at being able so clearly to remember them.

Gautama, who had been forgotten in the dimness of the unlit verandah, called to me, wondering at my slowness, and I went out, very inclined to take him by the hand and lead him surely up the steps into the night—though of course I did not do this. As we mounted the steps, a long dark figure suddenly sped past and, turning. I saw it was my cat, in a great state of alarm. Just then she reached the bottom of the stairs and paused, turning to stare back at me, her shocked eyes flashing in the dark, a swift, short beacon-flash of glinting topaz, before she disappeared, slender and silent, a beast of the night-time jungle.

'What's got into her?' Gautama enquired, for she had made him stumble and nearly fall. 'A guilty conscience, it seems. I wonder what she was up to on the roof, with those toms.'

But to this I had no reply. It was merely a distraction, a worthless comment that I did not allow to affect me, so that, if it was a pinpointed weapon, it glanced off my skin and fell, soundlessly. I continued to mount, step by step, to the roof, looking up to see the evening sky lowering itself to descend upon me till, suddenly, when I had burst out into the open, we were one—the blue immensity and I. Gautama followed.

I believe we strolled up and down for quite a while, as was our habit on an evening when we were alone, as, indeed, on most evenings we were. Now and then we paused at the edge of the roof, but not too close for the parapet wall was low, very low, low enough to sit on, quite comfortably, as the crows did, and looked over the stretch of gardens surrounding the bungalow, turning inkier and inkier, the shrubs and the trees, with not the life of day in them, but the uneasy life of a jungle at night stirring through them. The birds were quiet at last, each having found a perch to rest on, and the music lesson had begun. The high, tinny sound of the nimble sitar raced up and down the scales, too softly to irk, and the voice that followed it was too childish, too strained with effort to be mocked. Bats swooped across from end to end, lightning swift, but dark, and the small squeals they emitted might have been bits of stars tinkling to earth.

'They never get beyond the scales at all,' I said, not in complaint, but only as a statement of fact.

'Who?' said Gautama, who was smoking, with the preoccupied air that indicated involvement with a problem that his brain was grappling with in silence.

'Those girls next door,' I said, only slightly impatient, bumping into him to jog him into consciousness. But conscious he already was—only his mind revolved not in my world, but in his, a separate and distinctive one in which young girls striving to play the sitar and sing, bats nibbling at figs and flitting furtively

from one fruit to another, deepening darkness and
evening sounds, all faded so far across the horizon
that they disappeared entirely. Poor Gautama. Not
to be able to notice the odour of limes, not to hear
the melancholy voice singing somewhere behind the
plantains, not to have time to count the stars as they
came out one by one—poor Gautama, my poor, poor
husband. 'They practise the scales every evening,' I
told him, feeling so sorry for his lack of knowledge,
his inability to take interest, for it was this that made
him a grey shadow stalking, stumbling a little
ciumsily, a little lost in a world so full of very real
things. 'And I have never heard them play another
thing.'

'Slow, are they?' he murmured, stamping out one
cigarette after having lit another with it. This dancing jot of light at the end of the little white cylinder
seemed the only thing about him that was alive, a fine
antennae with which he kept in touch with the world,
however shakily He had not really heard the music
at all, and he paced on, even further into his desert
land. There was no way of holding him back from it,
and I let him go, further and further, in a dream myself, a vivid dream of surface sleep, in which colours,
objects, odours grew ever more vivid. The stars were
polished, shining in a clear sky, cool, deep and eternally lovely.

'Listen,' I said, stopping at a sound. 'Do you hear
that? It's an owl!'

He stopped because my interruption held him, but
he merely shook his head and paced on, a somnam-
bulist's figure in opium-white. 'It doesn't sound every
at all, does it?' I pursued, now that we turned from
206

the end where the garden lay to the end above the terrace. 'Just haunting—I like it in the dark.' He said nothing. We paced on, walked to the very edge, so that by craning one's neck a little, one could glance over and down to the grey level of the stone flags where a broad shaft of light from the kitchen door lay. Then we turned and strolled slowly across to the other end—some thirty paces or so—so that one could glance over our lawn where the two empty cane chairs stood near the stone urn that held drooping white flowers in the season of flowers, and fruitless, flowerless vines in other seasons, and the trees beyond, merging into the trees of other compounds, screening other houses, spreading into an inky pool to fade into the night sky that grew increasingly more brilliant more vivid than the sleeping earth. Again and again we walked this stretch till I was barely conscious of my foot-steps any longer, of turning at the parapet, though I felt disproportionately exhausted, and the backs of my knees began to tremble. And yet I could not pause, could not dream of pausing now.

But when Gautama held his silence too long, detached himself too completely into his exclusive mind, I drew him out again, finding it unbearable to lose touch of him. 'What *are* you thinking of?' I cried, touching his arm. 'You are so very silent again.'

He was startled at my touch and voice. 'Am I? Am I?' he said, and threw his cigarette over the parapet in repentance. 'It's this case, as I was telling you, and Krishnan. He is the one who is, for some reason trying to prolong it unnecessarily, and his intentions, I begin to suspect, are not quite honest. You see. . .' He began now to speak his thoughts aloud, not conscious of the listener at all, but eager to pursue the thread of logic to its end, slowly and steadily as a meticulous tortoise. I listened to him wryly amused, sadly so, thinking of how useless his words and opinions sounded in that palpitating night air, how petty and expendable under the gorgeous stars. Poor Gautama, poor dear Gatuama who was so intense and yet had never lived, and never would.

And then we turned again, walking towards the terraced end now, and I saw, behind the line of trees that marked the horizon, the pale hushed glow of the rising moon. I held him there, while I gazed at it watching the rim of it climb swiftly above the trees, and then walked towards it in a dream of love. At the parapet edge, I paused, made him pause, and his words were lost to me as I saw the moon's vast, pure surface, touched only faintly with petals of shadow, as though brushed by a luna moth's wings, so that it appeared a great multifoliate rose, waxen white, virginal, chaste and absolute white, casting a light that was holy in its purity, a soft, suffusing glow of its chastity, casting its reflection upon the night with a vast, tender mother love.

And then Gautama made a mistake—his last, decisive one. In talking, gesturing, he moved in front of me, thus coming between me and the worshipped moon, his figure an ugly, crooked grey shadow that transgressed its sorrowing chastity. 'Gautama!' I screamed in fury, and thrust out my arms towards him, out at him, into him and past him, saw him fall then, pass through an immensity of air, down to the very bottom.

Part III

It was nine o'clock in the evening, three days later. After a month of vacancy, the house in Lucknow had been opened up, its rooms aired, its lights lit. The servants, informed by one terse telegram of the arrival of the daughter of the house and the two women accompanying her, had been summoned out of their white huts behind the loquat and guava trees, and were now hurrying, partly through obedience and partly through animation acquired from the air of appalling scandal that had somehow infiltrated even into this monument to discreet and traditional aristocracy, like a significant snigger uttered at a solemn public meeting, to complete their work. Fired by enthusiasm, the gardener had even suggested working the old fountain again, but had been told, firmly and clearly, that this was not at all necessary, and that he must discard the notion altogether. So the three dolphins sprang into the air from a dry cement flooring, and no water spouted from their dust-choked mouths. But the library had been opened since the master was also expected soon, and four bedrooms aired and prepared. Yet, at this hour, it was as quiet as though everyone had fallen back into his summer-holiday attitude of repose again, though of course there was no hint of holiday lightheartedness. Its atmosphere was more like that of an expensive nursing-home for convalescents. So quiet was it that the very clock in the library seemed to move its hands with deferential slowness, like a funereal priest gesturing with sticks of incense and bowls of Ganges water.

The mother looked up every now and then at its bland face, then at her own wrist-watch, a frown darkening her face each time, as though she saw something she could not decipher, and this confused and troubled her. She sat in the semi-dark at the window that overlooked the tennis courts, and, since she did not need her eyes to knit, she kept her fingers busy with baby garments that she was knitting for a small orphan who had just been admitted into her creche as a special case, and who had not brought a single possession with her. The tiny fluff of the little jacket with its rim of pink looked entirely out of place in the grasp of her thick, knotted fingers and their quick, ceaseless, nervous movement, as indeed in that whole room with its atmosphere of hushed mourning and stunned silence.

When the clock chimed, Nila looked up too. She made no pretence of keeping herself occupied with handiwork, and sat trying to make friends with a dim-witted Pomeranian in between spells of dark brooding. Yet, when she looked across at her mother, she realized that that woman's occupation was no pretence and no shield. There she sat, counting stitches with the barest movement of her lips, as though the ordinary course of living in which work, hard and continual work, was the greatest part, and, at times like this, the only one, continued unaffected even under the greatest of stress. Nila noticed how her large, hard hands were absolutely under control, how they never dropped a stitch, how she never made an error, how the little garment grew steadily and smoothly without interruption. There was even a certain satisfaction in the face that bent over it, the satisfaction that came from imagining a child in it, warm, protected and safe. Yet there was no sign of absorption. There was too much tiredness on that face to leave any room for interest. Its tiredness made it dark, as though it had deepened, sunk to a so far unsuspected depth in which there was nothing but grim darkness. She held her figure erect, yet it was lifeless, weary, and a great strain seemed to go into the act of holding it under control.

Nila closed her mouth and sat back, poking the dog with her foot to bring it to life. 'Pomeranians are *too* stupid,' she said in exasperation, which made a small explosion in that hushed room. As the words fell on her own ears, she looked ashamed, screwed up her face, wondered if there were not something better to say. She finally said what was uppermost in her mind, though she wondered if it were not inappropriate and indiscreet to say it. 'The telegram hasn't arrived yet.'

'No,' replied the old lady. 'It hasn't. But from Switzerland it will naturally take some time. That is to be expected.'

'Yes,' Nila said, 'I suppose so.' She pursed her lips, then exploded again. 'It means we won't be able to leave for at least another week. It'll take him that long to get back.'

'Oh yes.'

'But I saw the servants opening up another bedroom this morning.'

A hint of vagueness overcame the harsh, steady

211

voice of her mother. 'There are so many rooms,' she said vaguely. 'This old house, it is full of rooms. So much room for my cre che. . .'

'How did they manage to live here—just the two of them? It's so—unlivable,' complained the girl, restless, uneasy. 'And the things that are crammed into it—a Victorian hodge-podge. It makes you itch to bring out a broom and a bucket. How could a young girl have borne it?'

'There was a brother too. The one whose letter we found in the desk,'

'Yes, the one she never told us about. I sent him a cable too.'

'Yes, that was right.'

They fell silent again, the younger woman in discomfort, the older woman out of tiredness, a disinclination to spend her last reserves on words, words. In one thing they were similar, and that was that in their thoughts, that ran much on the same lines, there was bitterness, naturally there was bitterness, but no hatred whatsoever. They followed the threads of the past three days slowly, having touched them often in the day already, and each time they stumbled upon the knots, the mysteries and, above all, the enigma of the blithe, child-like serenity of the girl, Maya, who sat somewhere upstairs, delightedly opening cupboards, pulling out drawers, falling upon picture-books and photographs with high, shrill cries of pleasure hugging them to her, dancing around the room with them, on air-borne feet. Now in the silence they could hear her moving above them, like a poltergeist, light and quick on its feet, eager in its chuckles of merriment, and frantic in its ceaseless movements, like a being

212

that is hunted.

'She hasn't gone to bed yet,' said Nila, heavily.

'No, she hasn't', agreed the mother, and immediately drew her lips down and frowned deeply at her handiwork, forcing her whole attention to it. Her voice was toneless, like the unbroken darkness outside.

But Nila could not listen to that happy, childish burbling with such stern equanimity. She would have given anything to silence that laughter, to banish the vision of that laughting, affectionate child who had met them at the door when they came to her in that still, secretive house of death. 'Don't you think the doctor might have given her a pill or something?' She said, with some desperation. Her voice was angry, but she was a large-hearted woman, an intelligent one, open to conviction. Only the conviction lacked! It was absent, so suspiciously absent. The stories that had been told, by the servants, and, in particular, Maya's own story, worried her as she reflected upon them in her restless inactivity. She stared at her mother, who had no such doubts. She had discounted the stories immediately, in particular the girl's. 'It was an accident,' she had announced, overridding them all with a fierceness that had silenced them effectively. But Nila could not accept this conviction with such fantastic completeness as her mother did. She was inflamed by the recollection of the girl greeting them with her feline embrace and, with a smile radiating out of her swallowing, brilliant eyes, insisting on bringing them tea, sweets, even as she recounted to them that story of mad horror, all in the same, cool, honeyed tones, while they had sat there, the

213

tea growing cold in the cups before them, watching her as one might watch a child play at soldiers and ruthlessly destroy them in its playfulness. 'So then I pushed him, hard, and he fell. And when I went down the stairs to the terrace, he was lying there— don't you like your tea? Shall I bring you lemonade instead? It *is* a hot day.' Nila gave her large head a shake, as though her ears buzzed. 'He should have given her a pill,' she cried. 'Or at least sent a nurse to stay with her.'

The mother was counting stitches and would not reply till she had come to the end of a particularly complicated row. Then she looked up and out of the window, into the darkness where her keen eyes could discern the white markings of the tennis courts, and the light at the gate where the gate-keeper sat, to keep away curious visitors who had heard, by the pigeon- post of rumour, of the daughter's return. She said thoughtfully, 'But the less people that see her and hear her story, the better.'

'Yes!' exploded Nila. 'Of course,' and flushed to think of that voice pattering nimbly through all the grim explanations of episodes unbelievable, as through a fairy story learnt by heart. 'Of course,' she repeated, so loudly that the dog started at her foot. 'But it will come out anyway, mother. You can't expect it not to. I'm certain she has already told others besides us—the servants, for instance, though we were lucky to catch that Pom-Pom person and send her packing. She looked just the sort who would have pounced on it as a juicy scrap of gossip.' She rattled on, angrily, but her mother barely listened, uninteres- ted in the doings and behaviour of people for the first

214

time in her active life. 'And even so,' Nila continued more gently, 'the doctors will have to be told once she's—there.'

She stopped short, in appalled embarrassment, almost guilty embarrassment, and her mother, sensing it, looked up at her in surprise, directing at her a lucid, piercing gaze of enquiry, as she had looked at the cruellest of realities. She was like an old, worn ship breasting the waves of a terrible but well-known and much-traversed ocean. Under it, Nila's confusion and embarrassment broke. She countered reality with reality, as her mother compelled her to do. 'At the asylum,' she said, softly. 'They will have to be told at the asylum when she is taken there.'

'It won't harm her there,' said her mother shortly, returning to her work. 'The doctor has already diagnosed her illness. It will be hard on her family, yes,' and her heavy shoulders shrugged very slightly, barely moving in the dark, 'It is hard for all of us,' she said.

Following this first confession of hardship, there was a long silence. The vast room, enveloped as it was by long shadows and pits of gloom, swelled with the rush of thoughts that filled both women now, in silence. With all their concentration, they still found themselves distracted, however, by the consciousness of the presence upstairs, of the girl with her round, wan face and soft featheriness of hair, explaining to them, in her coaxing child's voice, the details of the whole affair, of what exactly had led her to do it, her own purpose, her peremptory insistence that 'It had to be one of us, you see, and it was so clear that it was I who was meant to live. You see, to Gautama it didn't really matter. He didn't care, and I did.' Her smiles, her caresses, her calm certainty of their complete understanding. When they had tried to calm her and force her into her own room, to sleep, she had repeated, 'You *do* understand?' and then looked upon their horror with the blank gaze of those who no longer see reality. Then they had understood.

Simultaneously the two women recoiled from this memory, at which they had arrived together, and quickly turned to activity. They both had great faith in activity. The mother's hands flew about her wool and knitting needles in a blur, Nila busily unfolded a newspaper, folded it again, then began to read it, scowling. Immediately she lost interest in it, said, 'It's nearly ten. Why don't you go up to rest, mother?'

'No,' said the old lady, shortly. 'Not yet.'

'I suppose the servants have gone to bed, otherwise they could have made us some coffee.'

'Why don't you go and see if they are still up?'

'Oh no, it's too much bother. I don't even know where the kitchen is, or I'd make it myself.' She tapped her foot agitatedly on the fender. 'What do you think the children are doing now?' she said suddenly. 'Do you think they might be studying?'

'I should hope they are in bed, and sound asleep. Come here and help me wind this ball of wool. I've finished the white one.'

They sat there, knee to knee, but scrupulously avoiding contact, in the semi-dark beyond the ring of lamp-light, two black figures in bowed postures, jointed by a thread of white that each held in her hands and worked at, silently, absorbedly. Neither spoke, they dreaded speech now that they were so close together,

216

as though their thoughts and ideas, safe and controlled by each one within herself, would explode out of the bounds prescribed for them and spill into the open, were the two to meet and touch. They dreaded this as their son and brother had dreaded passion, as wise men dread their flesh. There was a certain fear in the tautness of their bodies, in the way in which they held themselves, and the way in which they stared steadily down at the wool which spun between their hands, flying from one woman to another, a dangerous live wire of connection, capable, at any moment, of ignition.

Strangely enought, it was the older woman who gave way first. She burst out, 'How am I to tell him? What am I to tell you father?'

Nila stared at her mother. The dark eyes, moonless, starless, expressionless, she knew, but there was some new horrible, senile weakness in that mouth that shattered some child-like faith she had had in her mother's invulnerability. The old woman was on the verge of—crying? Actually *crying*? She looked away, clung to the wool, not knowing whether to drop in and embrace her at last, or to keep to herself, leaving her mother to her private tragedy. She waited, biting her lips, and looked away.

Then the stirring summer stillness of the dark garden and the hush of the room broke. The sounds that had remained so far in the distance, now suddenly sounded very close, on the staircase perhaps. Both started, stared at the door, identified the sounds as footsteps, uncertain but swift, skipping and running down towards them. Then they heard the patter of a child's laughter cascading up and down the scales of some new delight

217

—a brilliant peacock's feather perhaps? Then it stopped, suddenly, and they heard a different voice calling, shrilly and desperately, from some unimaginable realm of horror, calling out in great dread.

The old lady was up on her feet first. 'Someone must go to her,' she said, and her quick voice was so low and reassured that the tenseness in the younger woman relaxed immediately. 'She is frightened,' said the mother, and hurried out of the room. Nila heard her climbing the stairs, pounding them in urgency. She rose too, and went after her to the door, where she stopped and watched the heavy white figure go towards the bright, frantic one on the balcony, screaming. They met for an instance, there was silence, and then both disappeared into the dark quiet. All around the dark was quiet then.

* * *

Raja Rao

Comrade Kirillov	15.00
The Cat & Shakespeare	15.00
Kanthapura	20.00
The Serpent and the Rope	20.00
On The Ganga Ghat	95.00
The Chessmaster & His Moves	275.00

"Raja Rao's talent for recording the Indian scene both town and country is vivid and unmistakably his own."
Deccan Herald

"Raja Rao is perhaps the most brilliant and certainly the most interesting writer of modern India."
New York Times Book Review

"Hurrah for you! You not only do India great honour, but you have honoured English literature by writing it in our language."
Lawrence Durrel

Nirad C. Chaudhuri

Scholar Extraordinary	30.00
To Live Or Not To Live	20.00
A Passage to England	25.00

"Nirad Chaudhuri is one of the most original and stimulating Indian writers today..."

The Observer, U.K.

"Mr. Chaudhuri is a born writer. He makes delightful reading, always thought provoking..."

The Times, U.K.

"Nirad Chaudhuri combines incredible erudition and a gift of style..."

Deccan Herald

"Mr. Chaudhuri is a serious writer with something important to say on aspects of life in India..."

The Statesman

"He produces his effects with the vastness of his knowledge, the splendour of his style, the energy of his passion and the loftiness of his tone..."

The Mail

Bhabani Bhattacharya

So Many Hungers	20.00
Music for Mohini	20.00
He Who Rides a Tiger	20.00
Steel Hawk & Other Stories	20.00
Shadow From Ladakh	30.00
A Dream in Hawai	16.00

"Bhabani Bhattacharya writes of Indians and the social, cultural and religious world in which they live with an authority and understanding that no Western writer can hope to match." **The New York Time**

"Bhabani ranks with some of the best writers of India in English." **Indian Literary Supplemen**

"Bhabani is a supreme master for interpreting rural India." **Nagpur Times**

Arun Joshi

The Last Labyrinth	14.00
The Apprentice	6.00
The Strange Case of Billy Biswas	20.00
The Foreigner	30.00

"Arun Joshi has evolved a style and thematic approach uniquely his own. His prose is at once as felicitous as it is flawless."

Khushwant Singh

"Arun Joshi is one of the younger Indo-Anglian novelists and he is also one of the very few writers who seem to be conscious of technique and technical experimentation, a very promising quality in a rising novelist."

Books Abroad, U.S.A.

KAMALA MARKANDAYA

A Handful of Rice   Rs. 20.00

This extremely fascinating novel by Kamala Markandaya makes the most absorbing and enjoyable reading. It depicts the hard struggles of life in a modern city and its demoralisation. Like her other writings this novel also portrays the struggle of a man to keep to the straight and narrow path towards respectability and economic stability.

"Certainly makes absorbing and enjoyable reading... the author has successfully and virtually captured the mores, the spirit and, above all, the lingo obtaining in the streets and by-lanes of India."

Indian Express

"An overwhemingly real book. It is about those part of us, as human beings, which are permanent and universal."

John Masters

"Shades of Pearl Buck haunt the description, situations and the characters."

Tribune

Dear Reader,

Welcome to the world of **Orient Paperbacks**—India's largest selling paperbacks in English. We hope you have enjoyed reading this book and would want to know more about **Orient Paperbacks.**

There are more than 400 **Orient Paperbacks** on a variety of subjects to entertain and inform you. The list of authors published in **Orient Paperbacks** includes, amongst others, distinguished and well-known names as Dr. S. Radhakrishnan, R.K. Narayan, Raja Rao, Manohar Malgonkar, Khushwant Singh, Anita Desai, Kamala Das, Dr. O.P. Jaggi, Norman Vincent Peale, Sasthi Brata and Dr. Promilla Kapur. **Orient Paperbacks** truly represent the best of Indian writing in English today.

We would be happy to keep you continuously informed of the new titles and programmes of **Orient Paperbacks** through our monthly newsletter, **Orient Literary Review.** Send in your name and full address to us today. We will start sending you **Orient Literary Review** completely free of cost.

Available at all bookshops or by VPP

ORIENT PAPERBACKS
Madarsa Road, Kashmere Gate
Delhi-110 006